CW00500381

FIVE   MOVEMENTS IN PRAISE

ALSO BY SHARMISTHA MOHANTY

Fiction
Book One, 1995
New Life, 2005

Translation
Broken Nest and Other Stories
Rabindranath Tagore
2009

FIVE MOVEMENTS IN PRAISE

Sharmistha Mohanty

almostisland

ALMOST ISLAND BOOKS
2013

Five Movements in Praise
SHARMISTHA MOHANTY

First published in India in 2013 by
Almost Island Books
11 Grotto Apartments,
St. Anne's Rd., Bandra (w)
Mumbai 400050, India
almostisland.edit@gmail.com
www.almostisland.com

ISBN 978-81-921295-1-8

Book and cover design Itu Chaudhuri

Printed at Silverpoint Press, Mumbai

Also from Almost Island Books
Trying to Say Goodbye by Adil Jussawalla

For K, always, always

TOWN

THE LAND RISES and falls, a geological breath.

It rises into low brown hills of bare rock, and falls in small brown valleys of loose gravel. A sky faded from too much light hangs very far above, unreachable. The sun plunges down from it, ripening rocks and gravel, brush and thorns. The traveler does not choose his landscapes. He takes what comes. Instead of a forest he may find a desert, instead of a pond with the tiniest fish he may find an ocean that has no end. Some will tell him that he may find what he needs instead of what he desires. And he will tell them that he has no desires left because they have all turned into need. His fears will travel with him, clinging to him with an endless love.

Each thing here, the rocks, the light, the soil, the heat, is hard and unbending. They equal each other in their devastating perseverance. The only things that seem airy and light are the shrubs that, seen from down below, seem to cling to the hillsides like gray brown clouds. But up above, when I touch them, they are as persistent as everything else here, rough, unbreakable, rooted so deep into the hillside that even if I pull hard at the lowermost parts, I cannot dislodge them in any way. In the land below the hills, there are a few emaciated trees with green leaves, and though they may throw a shadow they never give shade. This is the edge of the diminutive town.

Four mausoleums stand below the hills, made of dark brown stone. Here the stone has been carved into arched entrances, filigreed windows of stars, ledges with flowers and leaves running along them. Near these mausoleums is a white dargah that reflects and multiplies the light of the sun.

"Six hundred years," he says. "Shaykh Sharafuddin's dargah." The keeper of this dargah is a slim, quietly smiling old man. "And the mausoleums go back five hundred years. Some are generals, some are Sufis. They all wanted to be buried here near the Shaykh. Five hundred years...This is an ancient, sacred place."
The man's courteous body, bent ever so slightly and gathered inwards, now straightens gradually into satisfaction.
"Come," he ushers me in. His long, faded green robe is shapeless and too long. It sweeps the ground as he walks, gathering dirt and dust.

The courtyard has two rectangles of unexpected grass neatly trimmed, and on both there are several white graves. In between the graves, like the blooming of a sad pleasure, there are bushes with white flowers on them, the only flowers I have seen for miles.

The dargah is a small room, and so dark that my eyes take some time to discern the tomb covered with a green and gold cloth, the ceiling with sweeping curtains of red velvet edged with gold. It is a simple tomb, without any rose petals on it, in fact without any flowers at all, without ceilings or walls that are richly decorated. Everything is sparkling clean and neatly kept. There is a band of shadow thrown by the roof on to the white platform outside the room. I sit inside it, but if I move back even a little I will be in the burning sun. A woman in a burkha comes, kneels in that sun, and begins to pray. She looks down, with her covered face, at the ground beneath her, then straight ahead at the tomb, and finally up at the blinding sky, all the while saying her prayers under her breath. When she finishes, she throws back the veil on her face, shades her eyes with her right hand, and looks at me, as if she had been aware of my presence all along.

"Will you be staying long?" she asks.
"I don't know," I reply.
She looks around slowly, as if making sure the faded sky and the brown hills are in their places.
"We always have to kneel before darkness or blinding light, so that our eyes become useless," she says.
She lowers her veil and resumes her prayers.

The dargah keeper blesses me with the sacred broom. He asks me where I have come from. It is the only question he asks. I see in his eyes the most superficial curiosity, from which he wants to claim nothing. When I ask him his name the saddest smile appears on his face. He says his name is Rashid, with a long vowel at the beginning, which makes it different from the same name with the long vowel at the end, which means "friend", whereas his name means "the one who shows the right way."

I stand at the edge of the dargah, looking out for a long time.
"This soil..." I say.
"It grows no flowers or leaves," says Rashid, "because it gives rise to things more everlasting."

A group of young boys, perhaps thirteen or fourteen years old, stand on the broad ledge that runs around one of the mausoleums. They stand there as if surveying the land. They look down at me.
"The entrance is behind," they say. "But there's nothing inside except a grave." They are all thin and angular, their constantly darting eyes lined with surma. I ask them whose grave it is. They shrug their shoulders.

The large windows of the mausoleum are jalis made of tiny stars set in circles. The most delicate honeycomb pattern runs up the arched entrances. Inside, in the accumulated silence of centuries, there is a grave, on top

of which is a single, shrivelled marigold from a few days ago. Time is not even here, only standing still. As I watch, something falls from the high dome far above and hits the grave. It is a sparrow, and it lies there with its tiny head half severed from its body. The severed head rests on the marigold, both equivalent in their extreme lightness. A strong wind coming in through one arch could blow them away through another. But there is no wind. The bird and the marigold are fated to remain where they are till they become pared down, insubstantial, a past without its narrative.
An individual glance can revive nothing but itself.

Above the grave is the vast dome from where the sparrow has fallen. There a sudden, fragile turquoise can still be recognised, an indication that matter continues to be destroyed here, ceaselessly. But the jalis, created so long ago, are as potent now in the light of this present sun, allowing tiny points of illumination to hang suspended in the darkness. The light from the entrance is suddenly darkened. I see the boys gathered there, thin, dark shapes, with the sun behind them, curious to see why I am in here. With their coming time shows all its manifestations, and moves into eternity. But only for me. The boys turn their back on the darkness and go away.

———

WHEN I travel I never seem to gather facts, like a historian or a journalist, or a scientist. What comes to me are only facts that I already know. I do not seek new ones. But this time I try and collect some rudimentary truths. This town has a total of 2507 males that are employed, and 347 females. The average income is Rs.3,700. Some of these households have ten or eleven members. The larger the family here, the higher the income level.

Unskilled labour comprises 46.5% of the work force. There are construction workers, street sweepers, coolies, garbage collectors. A few beggars. The rest of the population is mostly made up of skilled labour—painters, electricians, welders, masons, bakers and potters. Some others are self-employed. In this category there are fruit and vegetable vendors, butchers, barbers, tailors, farmers. A very small part of the population are teachers, doctors, employees of the government.

There are no industries at all in this town.

The sun is low in the sky as I begin to climb one of the hills. The boys follow me for a while.

"Are you going to the top of the hill?" one of them shouts. "There's nothing there either." I stop and look back at them. They are quite close to me. I see in their eyes the same look that I saw in the eyes of the dargah keeper, a curiosity followed rapidly by resignation, a foreknowledge that what is new will never belong to them.

I pass a cave on the side of the hill. A middle aged man is sitting inside with his eyes closed, hands on his knees. I keep climbing. My red bandhni dupatta is delicate and keeps getting caught on the sharp shrubs, so I leave it hanging on a small bush, intending to pick it up on the way back. I reach the top of the hill and look at the orange sun. A vast range of low, brown hills spread out before me, in the sunset light. Below, the dry bed of what was once a river. Nearby, a mile or so away, Aurangzeb lies buried in a surprisingly simple tomb, a slab of marble. This simple grave was paid for by the Emperor with money he had earned from the sale of skullcaps that he had stitched with his own hands, and copies of the Koran that he had written out himself. Across the hills is a fort built by Muhammad bin Tughlaq. To the right, but not visible from here, the Ellora caves, where sculptors met the subcontinent's oldest rock, a volcanic basalt that offered the greatest resistance. From this came the volatile Shiva, the slaying Durga. As the sculptors overcame the resistance of the rock by understanding it, there came lovers leaning out into emptiness, and Jatayu flying through the air with urgent grace. This rock was formed from volcanic lava, at least 65 million years ago.

I hear a song coming from a distance. I turn around, and I see the boys standing far below, talking among themselves. A woman sits alone on a rock. The keeper of the dargah stands at his arched gate. The song seems to come not from below, but from far above. I look around me, it is a circle this song. When I have searched more than half the cloudless sky I see two people on top of another hill, I don't know whether men or women, it is too far to tell, but I can tell they are holding hands, and they are singing. I don't know whether it is a song of prayer, or of love. It travels down the valleys and up the hills, the only moving thing in this landscape. Just as I was beginning to learn from the hard, unbending endurance of the rocks and shrubs, the song comes. It is constantly moving, it is not the past but now, and it will not endure.

As the darkness gathers I climb down the hill. Looking for my dupatta I go around many shrubs but do not find it. Someone has taken it in the time that I climbed up and back down again. Perhaps the boys, to give a girl that one of them desires, perhaps the man meditating in the cave. Red is an auspicious colour for many things.

At the bottom of the hill the boys are still shuffling in place, displacing the loose gravel on the road, throwing a few pebbles far in a cricket ball throwing gesture. "Someone took away the dupatta I had left on a bush up there," I ask them. "Has anyone seen it?"
"We don't know anything about up there," they say. There is so much movement in these boys, but these movements actually consist of twitches and jerks of the neck, the limbs, the face, and the desire to move seems to be greater than achieved movement. A man stands apart by himself, a tall, broadly built man in a white kurta and salwar, with thick surma lined eyes. He looks at me directly and holds the look.
"You have to leave something behind in exchange for what you've received," he says. "The dupatta was from the softest cotton, a little transparent, bandhni in yellow and red. Who knows the many uses it can be put to?" His eyes slide down to the place that the dupatta would have covered.
"Tell me," I say, keeping my eyes on his. "I'm curious to know."
"It would be good to spread it out on the hard grass, to look at the tiny yellow dots whose outlines merge like little flames into the red, to lie on its

softness, and then to look up at the empty sky."

He knows that I will take something away from here, but he doesn't know what. His eyes are different than those of the boys or the dargah keeper's. They are very still, and in them there is no resignation.

"You could do that," I say.

"I could, but I'm not the one who's taken it. And then once someone lies on it, soon enough the sharpness of the thorns will tear it, in many places. Then it will have to change its function, it could become a rag for wiping things with, or it could be torn into thin strips, to make a wish at the dargah."

The boys continue to shuffle their feet on the gravel as they listen to the conversation. Rashid sits on his haunches at the doorway, above him the large arch of the gate, and weeps into the sleeve of his faded green robe.

"Saleem," he says, through his tears. "Saleem. No. No."

My interrogator looks at him once, and then looks away.

The song goes on, rising and falling, the darkness allowing it even more space than the light.

———

THE Sufis say that one travels for many reasons—to meet the masters, to learn, for self discipline, to achieve anonymity. The influence of travel on taming souls, they say, is no less than that of prayer, or fasting. The traveler knows that one can also travel only to experience movement when one is exhausted by that which no longer has any life. There is no curiosity, nothing cranes forward, not the mind or the eyes.

In the early morning I walk out before the sun rises very high. I see Rashid watering his flowers and grass. Beyond the dargah there is a stretch of open land. There is only one tree with thick knobs on the trunk, and three branches. One branch grows diagonally to the left, another winds over it to the right, and the third is so short it is almost a stump, angled downwards. Each of these branches bear a few thorns. Underneath it, as if it were a tree which was offering shade, there is a corpulent woman in a burkha, in surya namaskar. She is a middle aged woman with an almost masculine face. Her eyes are small and on the high nose there is a silver nose ring. I watch as she bends her knees and brings her hands together before the sun with an extreme suppleness and grace. There is nothing between her and the ground. Her knees and palms rest on gravel and stones. When I come closer I see that her entire body is trembling, a very delicate trembling like the leaves of a tree in a mild wind.

I walk by but she sees me. She sits down on the gravel, cross legged. The trembling stops.
"You're the one who lost her dupatta yesterday."
I nod.
Her face is full of suspicion. "Are you married?"
"No."
Her mouth twists into a vicious smile. "I thought not."
I keep looking at her, knowing she wants me to ask her the same question.
"I'm married," she says. "But I don't have children," she adds, her voice turning defiant.
She looks at the sun and joins her palms.
"Watch me all you want," she says. Then she spits out her disdain, a small thick mass of saliva that sparkles like dew on the stones.
Her arms rise above her, come down, she kneels, she is on her hands and knees, her head goes down and up again towards the sun, a continuing, tremulous flow, untired. I watch her for a long time, unable to move. When I do begin walking on, she looks back at me, over her shoulder.

A graveyard sprouts between two hills, plants and fruit of the barren ground, without any walls to mark its place. It seems ready to multiply in all directions, nourished by the heat, the cloudless air. Sitting on a tombstone is my interlocutor from yesterday.
"There is one more thing I would really like to do with that dupatta," he says. "I would like to cover my eyes with its softness and keep out this light

filled with malice. The perfume coming from the cloth, that smell of fading jasmine, would calm me, and maybe I would sleep, for at least an hour."

———

IT IS afternoon. There is no one here. I sit before the room with the tomb, and let my eyes get used to the windowless darkness inside. Today there are rose petals strewn on the green cloth covering the tomb. There is an almost imperceptible smell of roses. A dagger of light suddenly cuts through the room, falls over the tomb, lights a few petals. From where has it come? It trembles constantly as if reflected in moving water. Now there appears a small arched window on the back wall from where a different sunlight can be seen, as pale as that on a winter's day. The dagger of light catches the frayed silver hem of a robe, moving, and beneath it two aged, slim brown feet. I kneel on the threshold and look in so that I can see better. I see movements, a piece of green robe, a foot, a long, slender hand, all as brief as the flutter of a passing wing. For only a moment, I close my eyes. When I open them I see an old man in a green robe with a frayed silver hem, standing before the arched window. His back is towards me. Standing next to him I see, myself, holding a little girl in my arms. The little girl has hair full of curls, it is myself as a child. The man in the robe puts his hand on my head and strokes it. I stroke the head of the little girl who is me that I hold in my arms.

It is a childhood from the beginning severed from the child, a womanhood stopped short of itself, a serrated adulthood, forced and false in places, and in others luminous, capable of luring many things into its light.

The little girl begins to laugh. She laughs in the way that children sometimes do, without reason. As she laughs she turns her head and looks at me who holds her. The man in the robe takes the child's face in his palms. Then he gestures towards the outside beyond the window. I stand up to try and see what he is gesturing at. I can see nothing, the window is too high.

Now I can hear water flowing, somewhere outside the window. It is like a faraway river, but soon the sound grows louder and more full, a waterfall. As the sound grows the figures disappear, and then the window and the light. The room becomes dark again. Only the rose petals remain.

Rashid walks in to the room and that is when the sound of the rushing water stops abruptly. I close my eyes.

When I open my eyes Rashid is sweeping the tomb.
"You swept away the rose petals," I say.
His slim face undergoes a change as if it was being battered, the cheekbones rise, the skin is sucked inwards, the eyes are closed as if in pain.
"There are no roses for miles," he says in an angry whisper. "Once in a few months they come in from the city, looking as if they have already been on someone's grave."
He keeps looking at me. I turn my face away from him.
"Go away," he says. "Go. I have work to do here now. I'll be shutting the door of the dargah."
I am reluctant to leave. I keep looking into the small room, till Rashid begins to shut the door.
I do not know that I am walking out backwards, very slowly, putting one foot behind the other, slowly but firmly, without stumbling even once. Rashid continues to look at me, and I move back and back till the opening of the dargah is a black rectangle. When I have almost reached the arched gate, Rashid calls after me, angry, demanding, "Come back in the evening." It is only after I have gone through the arched gate that I turn around and face the outside. The late afternoon sunlight and the barren hills face me.

TIME goes so far back in this land that the traveler's questions sometimes have no answers. That frees him from actuality. It goes so far back that once he has experienced the force of a ruin, as well as the inevitability of its decay, he is left only with time's incomprehensible sweep, which will make his own life larger, as if it were space. It will not matter that he has not done all he wanted, or that he has squandered his time despite himself, or that parts of him have not survived. His grief will find its proper place, unlike in his daily life.

What will heal him is the many kinds of time that he will encounter —measured, immeasurable, the time of history and geology and tales, none of them the same. The only thing he may not meet is the future. But that will not hurt the traveler who is always moving onward, ahead.

This evening a wind has risen, at first insidious and curving, moving swiftly between the hills. But soon it swells and begins to spread, shaking even the stiff brush and thorns. Rashid sits just inside the threshold of the room with the tomb. Opposite him, right outside the threshold, sits the corpulent woman. Her back is towards me. The white light of the dargah falls over them like a grievous blessing. It is a light that takes away the beauty of evening, which everyone has looked forward to in the day. The woman and Rashid seem to be looking at each other. Somewhere a man begins to wail. The woman immediately bows down her head, and Rashid blesses her with the sacred broom. She walks away and he looks up and sees me.

He comes away from the white light inside the dargah, a light without shadows, without reprieve, he says. In the old days the lights were yellow, but the dargah committee brought in the white ones a few years ago. They last longer. A yellow light, can there be a simpler desire, he asks me with a calm smile. There is no anger on his face.

"Come," he says.

We turn our backs on the white light and make a half circle around the dargah and go to the low brick wall behind. Beyond the wall there is a large rubbish dump. It has been rising higher and higher over the years, Rashid says and perhaps one day it will be higher than the hills. Thin white plastic bags are the only things visible in the dump, because the moon lights them up with tenderness and the wind makes them swell and fall. For years, says Rashid, he has stood only on the other side watching the brown hills, or looking at the filigreed mausoleums outside the gate. Or he has climbed, at sunset, to the top of the old fort and looked around him, at the empty landscape, the sky. But he needs now, he says, to practice on things which are not beautiful, from which he can expect nothing. It is here that he stands every evening, thinking.

Rashid's skin is as smooth and moist as my own. It shows no signs of aging. Every day he tends the flowers and grass, he says. It is hard work keeping them alive. He cleans and looks after the dargah, arranges the qawwali on Thursdays, cooks his meals, goes to the market, washes his clothes, prays. It is not a hard life. But how does one crawl out from under the piling up weight of the years? How does one live within one's circumstance and not dream about any other?

He looks at me, as if expecting an answer. I have none. I stare at the rubbish dump. The fetid smell is hard to bear.

In my childhood I used to have a dream that recurred, I tell him. I am walking down a street next to the large gray house in which I lived in reality, its colours dulled by the sun and washed away by the rain. The street is also exactly the same as in reality, with the houses of my neighbourhood friends on either side. But, unlike in real life, there is an enormous heap of rubbish at the end of the street, the size of a small hill. In it is mud, loose soil, worms, coconut shells, rats, rags, mango peels, cooked rice and rotting vegetables, fish bones and half chewed fish heads. Standing next to it is a very old woman in a white sari stained with filth, thin, wiry, and with her matted hair knotted on the top of her head. She is toothless and she smiles at me. I know, with the kind of certainty one is given in dreams, that she is utter danger. She is waiting for me. I am transfixed, terrified, unable to move. I know I have to cross the hill of rubbish with the old woman next to it, I have to get to the other side. I cannot turn back the way I have come though that would be the easiest way to escape. For some reason that is not a choice open to me. The houses on the street are all quiet, no one at the windows or balconies, not a single person to help. That is where the dream ends.

The other recurring dream I had as a child, a companion dream, was this. I am in a deep green forest. I cannot see myself from the outside, but can feel myself walking through the dense foliage, parting it, the leaves and twigs touching my face, brushing my eyelids, flattening under my feet. As I walk, I see birds on the branches, not high up and far away, but close to me, close to my face, looking at me, singing, calling, a pie-crested cuckoo, a kingfisher, birds from other lands and continents, a red-winged black-bird, a cardinal, a red-headed woodpecker, on and on I walk, and the birds keep appearing on branch after branch, every single one different from the other.

"You dreamt of human life," says Rashid.

The wind has been intensifying all this time, gathering a sinister speed and force. It sweeps through the valley and over the hills making a great rushing sound. Rashid's robe flaps and billows.
"Come," says Rashid. "I don't want you to have to stand here."
As we leave there is the sound of a tree falling somewhere nearby. Suddenly the rubbish dump begins to crumble. The wind is separating all its elements with great speed. I see rose petals flying through the air and my heart moves in surprise, but then I realise they are pink, translucent onion skins rising high in the wind. After that there come cooked rice grains stained with gravy, a child's broken umbrella that opens as it travels sideways over our heads, a woman's torn slipper with a dangling heel.
"We should go inside," Rashid says, but he keeps walking, narrowing his eyes against the wind, and bending his head slightly.
"Yes," I say, but I only put my dupatta more securely around my head.
We reach the arched gate.

A large piece of broken mirror comes flying over the gate. It moves in a long arc, slowly, and then falls into the patch of green that Rashid tends, shattering immediately, throwing up tiny pieces of glass which settle on the bushes and plants like glistening dew. The wind swirls with rinds, shells, peels, everything whose insides have been eaten, it swirls with things torn, broken, crushed, pulverized, each thing without breath or destiny.

"I am sorry I told you these mausoleums are five hundred years old," Rashid says. Orange peels, mango stones, coloured threads, used rags, and a battered toy car travel by. Cooked rice grains coloured yellow deposit themselves on his hair, and a chicken bone with some flesh still on it slowly slides down his right shoulder.

"The truth is I don't really know."

"There is rice in your hair," I say. I step closer and stand facing him. Matchsticks rain down on us. Rashid does not look at me, he looks at the night. I begin to remove each grain from his hair. Some of the grains are stuck to his scalp. I have to hold them between my fingertips and slide them down the strand of hair to which it clings. It takes me a long time. I brush off a few matchsticks. Garlic peels float around us, like petals of jasmine.

The traveler may expect ruins, but not debris, not refuse. Nevertheless, he stands firm in a storm, even a tornado of rubbish. What can fell him is his need for love.

"Even this wind is on its way somewhere else," Rashid says. "Just passing through..."

What can fell the traveler are a few truly spoken words.

A black flower with its long petals drooping downwards, separated from the night only by its shape, moves across the darkness, spinning twice, before falling near our feet. It is a banana skin, blackened by decay. Night has taken away all the sharpness of this landscape, covering the scrub and the thorns and the barren hills, endowing it with a gentleness it does not have in the day. I look at the land's other self. At the bottom of the hills the night is most dense as it huddles together with shrubs and thorns and unknown forms of life that move only in these dark depths. The hills themselves have become continuous undulating shapes. At their ridge hill becomes sky only through a difference in tones. The hills are dense night, impenetrable, and the sky dark but with an infinite transparency. Far above, there are stars. They are more than beautiful.

The wind has brought massed clouds that move over the sky, and every time they appear the darkness deepens below. The mausoleums become part of the night when the clouds come, and become themselves again after the clouds have gone. Under the moving clouds I recognise the thin shapes of the boys, one of them brandishing a stick in his hand, lunging at the stormy air filled with useless things, perhaps, who knows, even at the stars.

I do not know any more whether to admire endurance or despise it, most of all, in myself. When is it that endurance turns infinite, and if it is infinite is it still endurance? The stars will not quench my questions. But they will do from afar what night and human love will do from nearby—make gentle the rough, make smooth the sharp, make invisible for a while that which does not have to always be under the light.

A dead bird comes flying, the wind forcing its wings open but not its eyes, spreading its tail in a fan. It hits the ground at our feet. It is a dead fantailed robin.
Rashid scoops up the fallen bird.
"Here, take it. My gift to you."
I cannot bring myself to take the bird in my hands.
"Touch it," he says.
I shake my head.
His jaw hardens. He holds my wrist and forces my palm down on the bird. It is the softest thing I have touched in a very long time.
"Why do you want to give me a bird that is dead?"
"There are live birds everywhere. Anyone can give you one of those."

We bend our heads, gather in our bodies, and go back to the dargah. I am holding the bird in my hands. The wind has forced open the old wooden door of the dargah and inside the spotless room there are now balls of hair, feathers and dust. I stand outside. Rashid looks at it all and steps in. He picks up a broom. A great exhaustion passes over his body and face.

"I asked you to come because I wanted to tell you," he says. "What you saw here this afternoon is seen only rarely. And that only by travelers, people passing through. Never by anyone who lives here." His face begins to tremble.

"Was there a dagger of light?"

I nod my head.

Rashid turns away. The sweeping begins.

I walk away with the dead bird in my hands. The clouds will pass by leaving the land bereft not of rain, but of movement. The storm will pass by without cleansing, and everything it has pried loose will have no choice but to settle again into the depths of this still landscape. So too this bird which I must leave in a place protected from the wind. I do not want it to be forced up into the air again. As I keep holding it my aversion ebbs. It offers feelings of flight, of rising, of breath. That is what it offers to one who is still alive.

The day after the storm, the sweepers are gathering the scattered rubbish into small heaps. All morning there is the sound of sweeping brooms over rock and stone and soil. Tired from the beginning, the sweepers pass over things, pieces of newspaper, a small chunk of meat. The onion skins escape them so easily that they lie scattered everywhere, as naturally as fallen leaves. Exhausted, the sweepers sleep at noon inside the dark mausoleums, or in the large, deep shadow cast by a rock. There are coloured shreds of plastic bags impaled on a tree of thorns drooping downwards, irredeemable leaves on destitute branches. Among them hangs my dupatta, soiled and torn, one end wrapped around a large thorn, the other lying on the ground. In the patch of green that Rashid tends, the white flowers lie crumpled on the soil, along with the stalks that held them, covered by bits of glass that glitter in the sun. In the ruins of a mosque the boys play cricket with tiny plastic balls and their wooden sticks.

I discover Saleem standing before a wooden cart piled with fruit. Incense sticks burn on top of the pile. As I am walking up to him I see him take an incense stick and burn a hole in a papaya, then in an apple. He has not seen me. He takes another stick, lights it and continues with the other fruit. Every few minutes he lights the stick again. The ground below is strewn with fruit peels, seeds, and matchsticks. I reach the cart and he immediately arranges the incense sticks back on top of the pile. The fruit are all haphazardly piled, papayas on top of bananas, oranges and mangoes squashed next to each other. Every single fruit is pock marked with holes. I ask him what the holes are.
"Insects," he says, looking directly into my eyes. The holes are tiny, but from them squeeze forth drops of juice, orange, yellow and white. Large black flies hover overhead and lunge at the holes when they can.

It is not only the holes that bring the flies. Each fruit is decomposing, in its own way, at its own pace. The banana is the simplest, with its evenly blackening skin. The papaya more complex, nuanced, in some places becoming a deeper orange, in others acquiring small gray sores, in still others developing large gray black patches. The sweet lime is losing its green and becoming golden like early morning light. Dark brown slowly covers the pear like an unexpected shadow. And in certain places every fruit has begun to give in, losing its precision, caving inwards towards its centre, some fleeing away from their cores and inflating till the skin bursts to reveal putrefied flesh. My eyes fill with tears. I wait a while to make sure that the tears do not reach beyond the edges of my eyes.

"Can I have a papaya? One without insect holes?"
Saleem looks through the three papayas he has.
"No, none that the insects haven't touched."
"Alright, I'll take one anyway."

He wraps it in a soiled newspaper and hands it to me. As I give him the money he touches my open palm and begins to caress it. He looks and looks at my palm as if he is studying its lines.

"The softest thing I have ever touched..." he says. He goes on and on till I feel compelled to take my hand away.

"Why?" he asks.

I shake my head.

He looks at me. I turn my eyes away.

Then he turns his back to me. He kneels down amidst the fruit peels and shells and begins to pray. I watch him for a few moments and then look at the brown hills and the empty sky. How brown the hills are and how empty the sky. I find nothing on which my eyes can rest.

"The sun," Saleem says, rising slowly. "It burns my patience to ashes."

WE ARE on one of the upper levels of the old fort, Rashid and I. Through the stone arches we look out at the land. Across and around us are the

27

brown hills, and because they are low they do not interrupt the endless sky. The hills are brown, the sky without colour, the light static. It is distance and space that are the forces here, they offer themselves for consideration. Down below, the mausoleums, the dargah and the few houses attain a kind of fearlessness which I have missed in them face to face. They challenge the difficult land. Rashid says he comes up here sometimes, because it is the opposite of down below. One needs also the opposite of what one lives. He imagines that the old hunter gatherers needed to stay in one place sometimes to understand the long work of growth and flowering, and the very precise consolation that lies in recurrence. And farmers needed to leave those consolations sometimes so that they met an unexpected light, a surprising soil. Perhaps lovers need hate and anger and destruction. Not that he knows for certain, he has never been in love. So he comes here, he says, away from his daily life where everything is close, the tomb upon which he rests his head and prays, the flowers that he waters and grows, the worshippers he must bless, the dust under his feet, the food that he cooks and then eats. Up here, how can he explain it, the air and space lighten his responsibility to himself. He has come to believe that is one of the reasons the sky exists. Here both his ampleness of time and his solitude become enormous, and precisely because of that he understands the harsh, unforgettable gifts that they bring. Up here, he never despises his life.

Rashid sits at an arch and looks out. I walk from arch to arch and what I see does not change. Brown hills, a sky without colour, a sky without colour, brown hills. In one arch I come upon the flank of a hill, so close I feel I could reach out and touch it. It has small green shrubs growing on it, and in between the shrubs I think I can see a bird moving. After the hill the landscape falls away again, in its usual emptiness. The nearness of this hill changes things. That bird moving in the shrubs is a parrot. What is near can be relied upon in a different way than what is far. The parrot's perturbed call tears at the deep silence. This hill is unconditional, a natural truth. Darkness advances towards us across the sky, and blurs the contours of everything. The hill becomes a looming form rising out of the evening, and I only a human shape. The hill offers its dark flank for me to stroke. My hand moves over the hardness of its rock, the sharpness of its green scrub, though it does not. My palm is scratched by a point in the rock, soothed by the parrot's back, entered by the tip of a thorn in the scrub. I could also lay my head upon the flank if I needed, and recount my fears to the hill. Both of us know how to endure.

The traveler knows that the landscape is never a metaphor, it does not stand for something else, but only for itself. He watches the land, and himself. He watches himself moving through the land. It is watching that he trusts. He is not an explorer. His courage is of unknown provenance.

When darkness has rendered the hill almost invisible I walk back to the arch I have left behind and find Rashid lying on the ground. I touch him on the shoulder and slowly he opens his eyes. He looks as if he has been sleeping. A smile, of sorrow and shyness together, passes over his face. You must have been very tired, I say. He shakes his head. It is the longing for a hand, he says. He speaks so softly that I have to kneel down next to him. On his head a hand, stroking, he says. And he has to sit down, wherever he is, he has to turn away from tomb, sky, horizon, towards himself. He can feel how the hand would begin at his forehead, touching the bare skin. Then it would cross the forehead lightly, coming onto the hair and the head. This crossing would be significant, because the hand on the forehead was only a beginning, a concentrated anticipation. Only when it came onto the head would he feel he had been really touched. It was a hand of extreme personal attachment, unconditional. The hand would bring alive the roots of his hair, his scalp. His blood and breath would begin to move, going down all the way till his feet, then move back up again. The hand would stop at the hollow where the head ended and the neck began. It would return to the forehead and begin over again. Over and over and over, till everything that lay inside him without moving, these awakened and rose, and he felt freed from the stillness of this landscape and its extension, the stillness of his soul. But there is no such hand.

Rashid did not know what exactly happened after the longing overtook him. Often it came at a moment like today when he felt he had located the meaning of his solitariness, that he was learning at last to love time. He would find himself lying in the place where the longing had come, his body overcome by exhaustion. When he opened his eyes the universe seemed more distant, more slow, and without the capacity to inflict pain.

When we walk down the steep, winding stairs of the ancient fort in the gathering darkness, the bats flying over our heads, Rashid refuses my arm as anchor.

Down below the boys have finished their day long game of cricket. We can see them as we walk down the hill. It almost seems like they are waiting for us. An animal howl cuts the still air. We reach the boys and find that they are throwing stones at a dog, as brown as the gravel and the hills. Is there no other colour here? The dog howls and cowers, but it does not run away. The eyes of the boys have a narrow range, moving from resignation to boredom at times, only sometimes reaching the edge of melancholy. There is nothing that they love, man or animal or landscape. Again, they hit the dog with a stone, it howls and howls, moves only a little, but does not run away.
"They are not boys," Rashid tells me, "they are men, stunted and deformed."
He enters the circle they have made and picks up the dog in his arms and takes him away. The boys barely look at him. Their eyes are on me, a boredom lightly interrupted.
I walk away from them, their eyes on my back.

On another continent, very far from here, there is a small town. On its edge is an ocean, never anxious, never tired, and so clear and blue that one can see the coral and the weeds below. The cliffs that surround it are green with trees, flowers climb the walls of houses, and on the hillsides away from the ocean, the sun, never too harsh, looks after the rosemary and basil growing among yellow wildflowers. There is no poverty here at all, neither of beauty nor of material things. There are young boys here too, alone or in groups, riding a skateboard, taking home a loaf of warm bread, with an identical look of resignation in their eyes.

The next morning when the sun has spread itself evenly over everything and I am walking towards the dargah, I see the boys standing outside the gate. They have surrounded Rashid. I can see one of them pushing him with a force that throws Rashid backwards and down on the ground. They look down at him. He picks himself up slowly. The dog that Rashid had taken with him yesterday stands next to him and weeps. The boys move closer, as laconic now as always, utter silence among them. As I begin to run towards them one of the boys raises a wooden stick and brings it down on Rashid's right shoulder. I reach him and see the blood blackening his green robe. They push him again and this time when he hits the ground he does not get up. His eyes are shut. Saleem comes up from behind the boys and I know that he has been watching everything. Now he picks up Rashid in his arms. The boys say nothing. Perhaps, for them, each action is perfectly equal to another, the stoning of a dog, the beating of a man, a conversation, a game of cricket, the beaten man being carried away. Saleem takes Rashid inside, to his room. I am about to enter the room when a woman rushes in before me, weeping. It is the woman I had seen sitting with Rashid at the dargah. Saleem appears at the door and says, "Please come back later. We will take care of him."

I wait outside the arched gate all day, sitting on a rock. It is the first time that I have sat under the open sky here like this, for so long. The sun reaches its zenith over me as it does over tree or house or hill and then declines. A man walks in with a bag. He seems to be a doctor. After an hour he walks out again. I try and read his face for signs, but ask him nothing. He looks at me as everyone does here, with curiosity but also with a knowledge of my irrelevance. At the hour of sunset I hear a song coming from the top of the hill. Once again I cannot tell whether it is a song of prayer or of love. The traveler knows that cause is a false home. That if you begin to unravel the cause of anything it will not be like a thought or a cloth but like a river at its source which has just begun to flow and very soon will carry along all that it meets on its way, flowers, corpses, and gods.

Saleem comes out.

"You can come in now, he's better."

I go in to Rashid's room, already bathed in the white light that he has fought against and lost. He is lying on a low bed, and the woman is sitting next to him on the ground. She looks at me and does not ever seem to take her eyes away. I sit down on the opposite side. Before I can say anything, Rashid says, "I'm alright. Please don't be worried."

I nod and sit silently for some time, as silent as I had been on the rock outside. The room has nothing except a clay pitcher of water, a steel glass, a Koran and a prayer mat, so old and knelt on that only some broken outlines of the original image are left.

"Is it very painful?" I ask.

"Yes, but bearable."

I stand on my knees and put my hand on Rashid's forehead. It is burning with fever. I begin stroking it.

"Do you see how we live here? Between prayer and slaughter."

I nod my head again. Across the bed, the woman is weeping quietly. I know why. I walk across to her side of the bed and sit next to her. She turns sideways to look at me, surprised. I take her hand and place it on Rashid's forehead. She takes it away so quickly it is as if she had touched fire. She begins to weep loudly now, as if heartbroken, and leaves the room without looking at anyone.

"You shouldn't have done that," he says. "She's a married woman."

I close my eyes. "You have lived too long with ruins, with tombs," I tell him.

"And what," he says, "would you have us do?"

There are tears in Rashid's eyes.

"That is not what I meant to say..."

He nods his head, but the tears have crossed the edges of his eyes.

I put my hand back on his forehead. He puts his hand on mine that is on his forehead. Slowly, he falls asleep.

A light is on inside the dargah. I hear a sound of tearing cloth. When I reach the dargah I see the woman sitting at the threshold. She has my ruined, torn dupatta in her hand. She tears the cloth with her teeth at one edge. She is still crying. Her teeth are small, pointed and sharp. She rips the cloth all the way down to the other end. She attacks the cloth with a fierceness far greater than what the cloth deserves, in the way that people sometimes will, unleashing their grievous anger on to the most helpless, inanimate thing. She tears the cloth into the thinnest strips. She stops crying. The sound of tearing cloth becomes softer, slower, less discordant. "It was already soiled and torn by the storm," she says to me. "I didn't think you would want it back."

"Do the boys ever come to the dargah?" I ask.
"No. They don't need to yet," she says. "But they will, sooner or later. What else is there?"

———
A GROUP of ten men have come to pray at the dargah. After their prayers they move backwards slowly. They look over their left shoulder every few moments to make sure they will not stumble against anything behind them. But that looking does not distract them. When they turn back towards the room's dark opening, their faces are as quiet, their eyes steadfast. I know, as surely as something proven, that this ritual comes from a very true source. I too have finished my time at the dargah and walk backwards. But I am less practiced than the men. So I have to stop and steady myself every so often. The boys appear from behind the dargah and watch us all. They have their back to the room with the tomb. As we go back, they come forward, facing us. The men do not seem to notice. We go back, the boys come forward, till we all reach the arched gate. If one passes on rituals one must also pass on a fragment of the immensity that produced them. The boys keep coming forward, one of them repeatedly throwing the wooden stick between his two hands.

I stop outside the gate. The boys stop in front of me. They are looking at me, but their eyes keep moving to other things, and coming back to my face, my body. They can rest at nothing, these eyes, not the hills, the sky, or a person's face. Perhaps, for them, there has never been anything worth looking at.

FOREST

THIS IS NIGHT where lovers, gods and travelers walk without a lantern. A luminescence separates the clear ground from the tree trunks, the trunks from their leaves, the leaves from the sky. The foreground of the forest is shadowed, but over there, beyond the trees, the land curves in an arc like a horizon, and the luminescence grows into a pale silver light. That is where he wants to go. So he begins to walk through the dark blue night between the tamal trees, each one of which is curved in a different direction. Next to one tree he sees Radha and Krishna, entranced by each other. Radha's open palm, angled towards the ground, shows the way home. But her legs are crossed one over the other as she stands, and her right foot rests firmly on the earth, her face turned in exactly the opposite direction to the indicating hand, towards Krishna. The traveler passes them by, but in his eyes there remains an imprint of the way their bodies curve, always outwards, touching the night, and next to them the tamal, leaning away from them. The reticent golden glow that illuminates their bodies from within lights up the left side of his face and shoulder as he passes by. The traveler can feel the glow on him, but it is towards the pale incandescence beyond that he moves. Already he feels it is something he recognises.

The traveler is not in search of adventure, the wilderness, endless cities. His travels are impelled by an extreme necessity, the need to save his life, from the inside out. The body has never been in peril, but his life, his life has. If his body were imperiled, his walking feet would feel the scratches of thorns, bleed from the sharp points of rocks, get blistered from the surprises of landscapes. But what he feels instead are the textures of moss, mud, seashore, pebbles, sand, grass, puddles, flowing water—he loves them all—and he pays attention to what each of them gives to his feet, where all the nerves of his body end.

This forest, he has seen nothing like it.

He continues to walk through the trees till he reaches that place of luminescence. There are no more tamal trees here. Two tall palm trees stand together, and one a little further away, alone. Beyond, there are dark hills. The traveler looks up and sees very few stars. Then he knows this faint glow comes from the entire upper atmosphere that surrounds the earth. It is created by reflected starlight, moonlight, man made ultra violet rays, and molecular processes. When seen at night it is called nightglow. He knows that scientists have been measuring nightglow, sometimes by sending up instruments in helium balloons which move around the world over a period of fourteen days.

He looks at the light which is itself, not a means to looking. It does not confer clarity on things. He stops walking. He sits down, then lies back on the ground. This light has taken away his will, given it time to rest. It is the first time he sees how much will a traveler uses up. He looks at the light. It is an extreme serenity, but when it falls on him it does so with a different, immeasurable consequence. It pries things loose, makes them rise and shift, and brings to the consciousness movements never before felt.

He hears laughter, and when he opens his eyes he sees a little girl looking down at him. She stops laughing all of a sudden, and says, "Are you lost?"

"No," he replies, sitting up.

"You're lying," she says, her voice curving on the second word.

"And you?"

"I'm just playing."

"By yourself?"

She nods her head.

"It's possible here," says the traveler.

"It's possible everywhere," she says. "Let's run."

She laughs as she runs, in the way that children have, without reason.

She stops and stands close to him. She smells of fruits and leaves and mud. "Do you like this light?"

"It takes away my fears." He reaches out to take her hand. But she moves away.

"What kind of fears?" She bends her head to the left and looks at him. He cannot see her eyes clearly in the darkness.

"Many. The fear of being high up in an airplane. The fear of being shut in an elevator in a tall building. Who are you?"

She begins to laugh again. She runs, this time into the shadowed darkness of the trees. Her arms are spread out and she touches the tree trunks as she runs. She comes back, panting.

"This night shelters, it protects," she says, still catching her breath. She stands very close to him. She has large, dark eyes, black hair, brown skin. On her bare arms and her slender throat there are scratches, perhaps from thorns.

"Did you get hurt?" he asks, pointing at the scratches.

"Let's walk," she says.

The traveler stands up. The light falls on the ground after the line of trees and reaches till the edge where the land plunges downward. There is perhaps a gorge below, with a slender river, he cannot tell. The hills across are dark, and as he walks on this strip of light, he feels he is on an edge of the world.

"It will be so different in the morning," he says.

"There is no morning here. There is only what you see now."

The traveler continues walking, but he slows down. He looks at the girl, and reaches out again to take her hand. Once again, she takes it away.

"There have to be some places where there is nothing but serenity," she says. "Nothing but beauty and its strength."

He looks around him, as if to test the truth of this. There is nothing to prove it wrong.

"Where are you going?" she asks.

"I don't know. Wandering perhaps. Leaving things behind."

The little girl is quiet as they walk. A few moments pass and she stops. "Can you carry me?" she asks.

The traveler, surprised, bends down and picks her up with ease, and she sits light and slender in his arms.

"What is your name?"

She puts her arms around his neck. "Tara."

"The ground here is comforting, soft but firm," says the traveler as he walks.

"It is from the time that these hills and valleys came into being. What a time that must have been. To be present when something comes into being..." She is silent, looking at the sky ahead.

"This landscape is like a hand upon the brow," he says.

She points to a place where the land protrudes so that three sides drop away into the darkness. "Let's sit here," she says.

They sit down, and the little girl hangs her legs over the edge and swings them back and forth over the deep darkness below.

THE Museum Rietberg is on a hill. The traveler walks up from the main road, on to Gablerstrasse, a narrow, ash coloured cobblestoned street going uphill. Ahead of him is a low, gray sky, moving continuously with its clouds. It is April, and there are patches of snow on the cobblestones. Water from the melted snow makes the stones shine. On Gablerstrasse, the traveler passes the Villa Schoenberg on his right. The composer Richard Wagner lived here for some years. It was here that he composed *Tristan und Isolde.* Opposite Wagner's home is the Museum. It came into being as the home of Otto and Mathilde Wesendonck. They gave Wagner and his wife a home in the half timbred house beside their villa. Wagner had fled to Zurich as a refugee in 1849. He called this home "his asylum on the green hill." It was for Mathilde Wesendonck, with whom he was in love, that he wrote *Tristan und Isolde.* He gave her the draft score on new year's eve 1857, with a poem dedicated to her.

"Full of joy, empty of pain, pure and free, forever with thee."

In a letter to Franz Liszt, Wagner wrote: "Never in my life having enjoyed the true happiness of love, I shall erect a memorial to this loveliest of all dreams in which, from the first to the last, love shall, for once, find utter repletion. I have devised in my mind a *Tristan und Isolde*, the simplest, yet most full blooded musical conception imaginable, and with the 'black flag' that waves at the end I shall cover myself over—to die."

In Wagner's *Tristan und Isolde* the world of day is the world of unreality, where the lovers must deny their love. The realm of night, in contrast, is intrinsic reality, where the lovers can be together, where their desires reach fulfillment; it is the realm of oneness, truth.

Details come back to the traveler from the days of his adolescence when he learnt the music of the great European composers. He stops for a moment at the gate of the villa, a black wrought iron gate locked with an enormous padlock. He looks into the grounds, which seem darker than the street, as if many more shadows have gathered there. He sees a stern, black bust of Wagner on a white pedestal. Somewhere, as his life moved into adulthood, the traveler turned towards a different music—he began learning to play the rudra veena.

He enters the gate of the museum. On either side of the wet road plants have begun to awaken and sprout. In front of the villa is a tall, lean man with a kind smile. They greet each other. The traveler sees that the museum is two buildings, one the main villa and another a smaller villa, some distance away. In their entirety, the man tells him, the grounds cover 67,000 square metres. The two men walk past birch trees and fir, patches of water under the trees, they enter the villa, go down in a small elevator directly into a vault with steel drawers and bright white lights.

There the tall gentleman brings out the paintings, one by one, hundreds of them. This is the largest collection of Pahari miniature paintings in the world. He begins from the 1300s, taking the traveler back to some of the sources of the paintings that both he and the traveler have found hard to live without. The traveler stands there for hours because there is no room for chairs in that space, and because he could not have sat down while looking at these paintings. "Are you tired?" asks the tall man once, and the traveler is so far from tired that it takes him time to understand the question. He knows these paintings were meant to be held in the hand and looked at over hours, and there before him right now is Raja Balwant Singh of Jasrota looking at a painting which his court painter Nainsukh has brought him, sitting with his legs folded underneath him on a wide, ornate chair, while dusk falls forever from the sky on to the trees outside.

But the traveler cannot sit down, not now, not in a vault, not in this time and age, not when he has come so far. Standing and bending his head towards the paintings is the only posture that seems correct.

And so he looks and looks at the paintings of love in its infinite gestures, of gods, kings and sages, ashrams and courts, palaces on the crests of hills, he sees solid colours and flat planes, the blurred archetypes of trees, the single white curve that denotes the river, he sees all this change into rounded horizons, paler hues, trees and flowers and plants that can be identified in all their real blossoming details and multiplicity, and the river swirling with its currents of water, fish raising their heads for a moment, once even a boat, and yet the immensity and the reticence of the paintings unchanged over centuries. He had not expected the quietness of colour that he finds in them, so much less bright than in books, so much more restrained.

They go up in the small elevator again and the tall man takes him to an upper gallery, where at one end, under a glass case, he shows the traveler the brush made of squirrel hair those painters would have used, the colour yellow made from the urine of a jaundiced cow, the blue from fresh indigo, and most of all the glowing, dark green jewel of beetle wings used to decorate Krishna's crown.

After this the traveler sits on a wooden seat placed before a large, arched window. He sees nothing, thinks nothing. He does not lean back. He remains at the edge of the seat. He begins to notice, very slowly, the mist that hangs outside over everything, gray with a faint silver light within. Birches with their slender white barks float on this mist, as if without roots, their branches still bare. He sees that the tall man has left him alone. The land is flat directly outside the window but after a few metres it begins to slope downward to the valley. A wind blows and shakes the thinnest, barest branches, some of them mere wisps of wood. It reminds him of a few strands of Radha's windblown hair as she waits in the forest. Perhaps the breeze comes from the other bank of the river, finding its way through the mango grove in which she sits. Now the mist moves and begins traveling westward. This is how things are placed next to each other now, without warning, geographies and times buttressing one another. Down in the valley below, the moving mist reveals the slate roofs of buildings and the tall spire of a church, Zurich. His mind is flattened into silence, beaten down like a sheet of pure gold.

On his way out, he walks very slowly down Gablerstrasse. He steps with unprecedented concentration between the patches of snow, placing each foot firmly on the cobblestones, as if otherwise he would begin to hover over the ground. In earlier years the traveler had feet that would slip at the slightest moisture or the smallest pebble, he would often stumble, sometimes fall. But there came a teacher who made him stand, every day, with legs apart, knees bent, feet strongly on the ground. He said, "Now close your eyes and imagine your feet on grass, beneath the grass a firm soil, beneath the depth of this soil the first layer of the inner earth, then all the further layers, right till the centre, and then feel yourself standing, grounded, on the whole earth as it turns slowly under your feet."
When the traveler reaches Seestrasse, he stops and waits for a tram.

THE king has known great grief and so has come to the sage, the sage is a student of suffering, a prince is in an interminable exile, a lover is separated from love, yet everything is lit evenly, and there are no shadows, and so no sense of time passing, though of course it must, and there is a perfect warmth but no heat, no dust, no weeds, no decay. The traveler recognises this landscape of assurance, as he would recognise within himself a lifelong need never fulfilled.

He sees a man on a small raft, a student reading a manuscript. He stops to look at the sage and the king talking, sitting erect, looking into each other's eyes, only the king with a little more intention on his face.

Near the water, under the sky, the homes here are rudimentary, made of mud and thatch, only a shelter, a place to rest in. He is so silent as he walks that the little girl holding his hand looks up at him with concern.

"Is there something wrong?" she asks.

"Nothing, nothing at all," he replies.

In spite of the daylight that is always reticent, never changing, time is not invisible. The fruit has ripened (the present), the young man studies to someday understand (the future), the sage is an old man (the past), and the river does flow (a time outside the span of a human life). Time is present here, but not its ability to destroy. There is plenitude but never excess, the river holds itself forever between its banks, because excess would be akin to a fury, or an elation in which suffering would immediately show itself. Yet, this landscape is not restrained, it gives everything it has.

The traveler stretches out on the grass.

"You are wondering where anguish hides in this landscape," Tara says. She takes her small palm and places it on the traveler's forehead. He can smell her child's sweat. She begins to stroke his head, from the forehead, onto the hair and then the back of the head to where it touches the grass. Her strokes are even, uninterrupted. He falls into a drowsiness that reaches the edge of sleep. Tara's voice comes from far away, the words unconnected. "Unbroken sky," she says, "become many." And then, "Natural ripening and decay." Then, "Your own."

He hears her words, fragmented, but understands their indication. His fingers close around a few blades of grass, pulling them, tearing them up from the roots. He brings up his knees and holds them close with his arms. He turns with his bent knees and rubs his face on the grass. He turns again with his body bent forward now, his forehead touching the ground. He keeps turning in this way, holding every part of his body close to him, finding it impossible to open out.

There is a wind blowing, and it brings a few words with it, from the conversation between the king and the sage who are sitting under a tree nearby. "...on the throne..." says the king, and the wind dies down.

At home, if the traveler can still call it that, the street dogs snarl and fight in packs all night. They have been born inside storm water drains, and pipes, they are stunted and discoloured by lack of light.

"...but the kingdom..." says the sage, and the wind dies down.

"Not on the other side of the sky," says the sage, and the wind dies down.

After a sleepless night there is the deafening day. Marble is laid on the floors of apartments, buildings are built, cement mixers churn, stone is polished, drills vibrate all day, iron grills are fitted on windows, enormous glass buildings reflect the venomous sunlight, scaffoldings and large corrugated iron sheets grow on vacant lots, streets are concreted or widened, to reach the new.

"Not on..." says the king. The wind rises.

The traveler feels himself rising too. His body begins to open out, little by little, till he is stretched out on the grass once again, on his stomach, arms reaching out above his head.

"...he does not await the future," says the king. The wind continues to rise.

"Even if the sun does not shine..." says the sage.

"I'm walking on your back," says Tara. "On your spine." She walks up and down his body. It is pure pleasure and he feels he will surely fall asleep. But slowly, the footsteps become heavier, not so caressing, calling on his attention. He can hear his own breath, and if he listens carefully he can hear hers. Every step she takes is deliberate, careful. Where she places her feet, the nerves and blood rise to meet it. Wakefulness comes together with the relaxation of the body. Just as the footsteps become almost too heavy to bear he falls into a wakeful sleep. In his dream, in an open meadow glowing with light, the king is building a throne of mud and leaves. He takes the mud in his hands and creates one layer of mud, then he gathers the leaves and makes a layer of leaves, one on top of another. He never looks up from his work. The sage watches him. As the throne begins to take shape the rains come all of a sudden, violent and hard, darkening the meadow and reducing the throne to a lump that flows away in the water. The sage begins to laugh as they both stand there in the pouring rain.

When he wakes up the light is exactly the same.

"Did you sleep well?" Tara asks.

"Yes."

"I want to walk to one of those hills far away."

Walking towards the far hills they see the king and the sage on an undulating meadow. The king is building something with mud and leaves. The king has astonishingly small hands. His hands and arms are brown with mud, and in places there is a green layer over the brown. The traveler sees the sage becoming powerful and the king being stripped of his power and he wonders whether power is a pure energy which only changes form but never dies. At that very moment he sees the king smile.

They walk on in that light that never grows, never ebbs.

"What is it like now in the landscape where you live?"

"Now," he thinks for a few moments. "Now the rains would be ending, the clouds slowly retreating from the sky, the plants and trees will have grown tall and full between the buildings and in the vacant plot outside my window, yes some of the same trees as here," the traveler's voice becomes softer, "and in the lanes of the city the fruit seller will stand less tentatively not needing to watch for rainclouds, and the colours on his old wooden cart will be the orange papaya, the golden melon, green bananas, the pomegranate," his words are now slower, "yes the same colours as here, the same fruit."

He smiles at Tara, but really he is smiling to himself. What else is as continuous as light and vegetation and landscape, what else could reach across time and show a way to endure?

As they walk they see an emaciated man in a tattered green robe. He seems like a part of the leaves and branches under which he walks. He has the most slender hands and feet. He sees Tara and the traveler but pays them no attention. When a bird calls from a low tree, the man immediately stops and turns his head. He stands still and listens for the call to come again. They pass him by and climb the crest of a hill. There is a king on a horse, hunting in the valley below, with his soldiers nearby. They can see deer leaping far away. The king urges his horse on, faster, faster. They leave the valley behind and climb the next hill. Three men are resting at the top of the hill, their horses tied to trees. The traveler realises they have walked a long distance, but in this land of no heat, no dust, no weeds, no decay, he feels no tiredness. They begin climbing a steep hill. Before he knows it he sees that the sky has lost its sunlight. It is a low sky, like in a cold country where the sun has long been hidden. The land is losing its vegetation. It begins to get cold and he brings out from his bag a down jacket that he bought in Europe. He realises Tara only has her white chemise.

"Don't worry," she says. "I don't feel the cold or the heat."

Far away there appears a mountain range. Snow covers its peaks. The road becomes narrow, wide enough only for one person, and below there is a deep gorge with a river flowing. There are no birds any more, no trees, not even a plant.

"Where are we?" he asks.

They keep climbing higher, going, it seems, towards the sky. Suddenly the land opens out before them and he sees a group of trees to the right, the only trees in this landscape, their crowns full. On his left he sees eleven men wrapped in shawls but with their feet bare, looking ahead of them. The ones in front bend their bodies as if in asking, and some join their palms. The men at the back stand more straight, but in an attentive waiting. The traveler cannot see anything in the direction in which they are looking. He looks again but all he sees is emptiness, and the group of trees to the right.

"They are worshipping the absent Durga," Tara tells him.

The traveler cannot ask any questions, he has none to ask. His mind is white mountain air.

"Come," says Tara, taking his hand. "You are not meant to stay here for very long."

———

ALREADY, by the time he is ten, they have taught him, and he has learnt, to draw the simplest things. Eyebrows, folded hands, the outlines of distant hills. He is shaken awake one night and asked to draw, by the trembling light of the lantern, in the cold and darkness, a hand. He does it without thought, in a state between dream and sleep. "Not bad," says his father, Pandit Seu, and carries him back to the bed. By the time he is nineteen Manaku is drawing trees, the mango, the amaltas, he is drawing curving lianas on the trunks. He is lowering or raising the horizon. He is married, he falls in love. He wonders why there are no shadows in these paintings his family makes, no rendering of times of day, a changing light. He asks his father. "The answer will come to you," says his father, "if you wait." In the evening the men in the family talk, about a change in kingdoms, a gifted painter from another region, the swabhava of a colour. By day the women grind pigments—the finely ground lapis is for Krishna's body—men paint, and others in the family are building things from wood and iron. Manaku likes the sound of hammer on iron, or of wood being cut and sawn. He meditates at dawn, as his father does and his uncles. When he opens his eyes the landscape falls perfectly into place, hill by hill.

It is 1719. On the plains below the Mughal Empire is losing its life, the East India Company has been formed more than a hundred years ago. The British, the Portuguese, the French and the Dutch have arrived on all sides of the subcontinent wherever land meets ocean. Manaku is aware of some of these changes. He has already traveled, on pilgrimage to Hardwar, down to the Mughal courts on the plains. But in these hills time and history are not one. Manaku climbs a steep slope and a valley opens. He climbs another, and in the distance are the Himalayas breaking up the sky, reducing the horizon almost to the narrow width that he uses in his paintings. He studies horizons, their height and depth, different each day wherever he studies them. If love has turned into its absence, here is where he brings it, along with other things that cannot be spoken—the weight of a father's gift, the luminosity of a younger brother's craft. As he walks among the complex and unceasing rhythms of hill ranges and valleys, there is born in him on some days an elation so large and so strong that he sits for a whole day near a river without moving, or walks for hours over slope and valley. When he comes home, he hammers iron, to ground himself again. Or he sifts rice with the women, to bring his eyes back to what is minute. He paints the trees and Krishna almost the same height one day, by mistake, the trees only a little taller. His uncle comes by and stands there watching for a long time. This uncle is not a painter, his father's elder brother. He makes carved wooden tables for the kings, low stools for them to rest their feet. Yet it is to him that they all go when they have finished a painting. They trust his sight most of all. "I made a mistake," says Manaku. "No," says his uncle, "you have corrected something." Manaku watches the painting. He knows he cannot ask his uncle anything more. The elders do not like to use too many words. Over days he feels that once again, as with so many other things, his uncle is right. But he does not know why. Children are born to him, sons and daughters whom he loves. They will bring with them their own specific fates as he brought his. No one talks any more about Manaku being left handed. He paints King Prithu pulling an arrow with his left hand, once a gopi has a right palm on a left arm, and there is Krishna, painting Radha's breasts with a brush in his left hand. His patrons, kings and princesses, do not correct him, nor do his family. Who knows whether Krishna was indeed left handed? As a composition of human desires Krishna could have used either hand, and anyhow, what aberration had the universe ever excluded? When the pandits come he listens closely to the texts, the Bhagvata Purana, the Ramayana, the Gita Govinda. At the same time he sees paintings that have traveled up from the Mughal courts below, where landscapes are rendered in minute detail and every face is individualised, the way it is in reality. They paint always the real, these painters, they paint kings and courtiers, hunts, animals. He knows that painting the divine is forbidden them. He sees that from forbidding a thing, something else arises. His father, Pandit Seu, has absorbed elements from the work of the plains. He is among the first painters of the hills to paint vegetation in its details, to individualise his faces, to do portraits of real people. He has painted, in the same painting, the teller and the tale, and his brother will take it further and render at the same time the painter and his painting. But Manaku cannot bring himself to paint only a physical reality or to bleach it of colour like his brother. He looks at these Mughal paintings for many years, he thinks about them while drawing water from the river, putting a child to sleep. He rises earlier and earlier, long before the sun. He studies the night, before he sleeps, then again after he wakes up. He never paints night, but he paints the dark blue of Krishna's body. On one among his many nights of watching, it comes to him that Krishna is a fragment of night, a dark immensity condensed and thickened into a moving body, a god. He doesn't tell anyone. Speech exists to express daily things, as dear to him, but different. Tomorrow he will make the lapis a shade darker. This he can talk about, with his father, his brother. Often colours appear to him as he is about to fall asleep. The next morning he spends hours achieving the remembered colour, its exact tone and hue. They are solid planes of colour, monochromatic, haldi yellows, flaming reds, dark oranges, all of them aspects of sky. One day walking on the riverbank he sees the light change, the sun suddenly covered by one dark cloud. The light is now like that in his paintings, the hues of each thing in the land become less emphatic. After so many years he understands. That what he paints is outside time, what he paints is not a moment that will pass. That the movement of sun and shadow and light will introduce time and so inevitably its consequence, suffering. In the end what he paints is a landscape of belief, not doubt. He does not want to erase suffering, but he wants his paintings to hold it like the hills hold their ore. He bows his head and touches the ground. Next to him the river flows on. Flowering shoots as in the work of the plains enters his work, they stand alongside his stylised trees, and later comes an open landscape of undulations with green shrubs. He is very cautious when he introduces these physical realities, as if they would disturb an elemental reticence. But he is amazed to see that it remains, untouched. This silence, like that of an oil lamp in a windless place, he does not know from where it comes. He knows it is there in the work of his father and his brother. It does not come from the way the brush is held, it does not come from the colours, nor from what they paint. After a painting is finished, he watches his own silence within the borders he has just painted, like an outsider. His father dies, the great painter Pandit Seu, a daughter is given in marriage, his two sons sit bent over their painting. If one is fortunate, Manaku thinks, then time unfolds and reveals more than it seals up. When he is painting the laconic light, or perfecting the singular blue of Krishna's bare body, a power begins to manifest inside him. It is not a power over anything. It makes metaphors crumble in his hands. Finally it eats and digests him. He is left like a rind on the soil, not fit for human use. He lies motionless for hours. After this he chops wood. He grinds wheat. What is it that a painter paints? It is not beauty. He has taught his sons well, Fattu and Khushala. He has grandchildren. The absence of love in his own life becomes presence once again. He paints a Radha and Krishna, seeped in vermilion. The background vermilion, as if a flaming sunset sky. Radha's clothes vermilion. She sits on Krishna's knee. Before them is the white curve of the river. They look, not at each other, but to the right, both their faces held at exactly the same angle, they look into a distance of endless space. The trees have remained as he painted them in his youth, only a little higher than the seated Radha and Krishna. It was the mistake that made him see, slowly, that brought him to a belief he never had before. That each thing in his painting was equal, as it was in the landscape in which he moved, none diminished by the other, freed from a hierarchy imposed only by the eyes. When Manaku is cremated the light is like the light in his paintings, always forgiving.

They put his brushes next to him, and among the flowers his pigments, ground lapis, powdered vermilion, and strewn all over, the green beetle wings he would always use for Krishna's crown. The fire burns for a long time. It is 1760. What Manaku does not know when he dies, what he cannot know, is that the generations after him will perfect that light, that it will remain shadowless, but will have an even more subtle refulgence, that hills and rivers and horizons will open continuously, trees, plants and birds will get more and more detailed, and yet none of these things will impinge upon the elemental reticence, and his sons and grandsons will do something he had never done, they will have the courage to paint night and render it dense yet transparent, night of love never night of fear, and the dark sky will be filled with such a quiet nightglow that no one will need a lantern. After a few generations the paintings will, like any living thing, begin to decline, grow overripe. But that original light, and that original darkness, will reach across hundreds of years to another time, to solitary people sitting close to them in crowded cities, that seeds gathered by a Dutch merchant at the Cape of Good Hope in 1803 have germinated in the year 2006, and among the plants which have blossomed is Leucospermum, a rare, stunning, pin-cushion like flower.

THERE are no airplanes in this lapis sky, nothing made by man. When he thinks of airplanes he remembers the texture of his fears, in spaces that shine with steel and a sterile smoothness, spaces without moisture, without dampness, without sweat, without warmth, without a single golden light, without shadows, without wind. He feels trapped there, short of breath, broken. It is, he sees now, the absolute opposite of this landscape that is open, moist, warm, without purpose, immense. He never wants to return to those other spaces again. He is not afraid of change, of the breakdown of one's own heart, of the loss of love, but these spaces terrify him.

Tara puts her head on the traveler's lap. They have returned to the grove of tamal trees and the luminescence beyond. He caresses Tara's shoulder and her arm, feels the unfathomable smoothness of a skin barely touched by time. He strokes her, and she slowly falls asleep. He takes her in his arms and places her very carefully on the grass. He lies down on his side, next to her, his right hand on her arm. He thinks of his home, if he can still call it that, in the city where he lives, the building windows lit, the dishes stacked neatly in stoic metal dishracks, sometimes a rack surrendering and becoming concave from years of stacking, a child studying under patient lamplight, a hand moving over the even more patient bedsheets. Once, in this seaside city, a ship ran aground. It remained stranded in the mangroves for months, and the rust slowly spread all over its enormous shape.

Before he knows it he is asleep. He dreams of the same landscape in which he is sleeping. In his dream a cripple appears, a man with only two stumps below the waist. The cripple looks around him, calmly. With great skill and rapidity he drags himself towards the dark edge of the land. There he waits for a moment. Then he jumps across the wide darkness to the other side, where the hills begin, drags himself over the land and disappears into the night. The traveler is incredulous in his dream. "Even a cripple…" he says to himself. When he wakes up, Tara is already awake. She is sitting close and looking at his face.

"I wish you didn't have to go," she says.

"I'm a traveler," he says.

"I know," she says.

"And you?" he says.

"That cripple in your dream is my father." She sees the surprise in his eyes. "I did have a father and a mother, once."

"What happened?"

"I don't know. Perhaps they died. Perhaps they went away and had to leave me behind. Did you know that little children, even if they have food and shelter, can die from lack of love?"

The traveler shakes his head.

"Sometimes, when I shut my eyes and concentrate I can see myself as a baby, before the consciousness of sorrow or joy. Can you do that?"

"I've never tried."

"You've never had to try."

The traveler is silent.

"Listen. I was forced to look for life in everything. Slowly, I found it. It is power without intent to power. That is why it can appear in me, a little girl.

I may be one of the most powerful people you will ever meet. Look at me, look at my eyes."

The traveler raises his head.

"It is power that cannot be broken, because it cannot be learnt, or studied, or replicated. It occurs in your world too."

The traveler cannot turn his eyes away from Tara's face.

"Those who have power," Tara says, "but not over anything, are the ones who hold up the world."

She walks towards the edge and sits down, swinging her legs over the darkness below. It seems like the night moving, back and forth, in a corner of itself, calm but defiant.

She raises her arms and begins to plait her hair into a braid. She brings one strand carefully over another and the gestures of her fingers seem to push her towards womanhood. But of course she is not yet a woman, not yet even a young girl.

"How do you know your name is Tara? Do you remember being called that?"

She finishes braiding her hair and turns around. The defiance has moved now into her eyes.

"No. I gave myself that name."

From the tamal grove, two men emerge, glowing in white clothes. They are young men and when Tara sees them, she gets up and runs towards them. One of them picks her up in his arms and strokes her head. When they reach the traveler she tells him, "They are storytellers. They come here to think, to create new stories that they will later tell." She runs up and down inside the luminescence once again, in joy, laughing.

The traveler feels forgotten. He feels an unfamiliar envy of these storytellers. "I will be leaving now," he says.

"Alright," she says, stopping her running for a moment.

"Come here."

Tara comes to him, and he goes down on his knees.

"Yes?"

Very hesitantly he stretches out his fingers and touches her on the right arm. He feels both the softness of her child's skin and the rough, raised line of a scratch.

There are places you want to be in forever. But the way of those places is in their extreme compression. They will always exist but you must pass through them and out each time. They are not meant to hold the elongation of a life. He shuts his eyes and gathers Tara in his arms. For a brief moment he smells again her smell of sweat and leaves and mud. She frees herself very quickly and runs to the storytellers. She sits before them cross-legged.

"Tara," says the traveler, one last time.

She turns around with a smile on her face, but only for a moment, before she is engrossed in her friends once again, like a child, for whom the past, and everything in it, is as evanescent as breath.

———

THE traveler winds his way back between trees, guided by the nightglow. He comes to a clearing, and then suddenly a river. Fallen mango leaves soften its banks. Once again he sees Radha and Krishna, this time sitting on the bank, facing each other. Krishna leans forward and holds Radha's right wrist with one hand. With the other he holds her left foot. The traveler studies these gestures that have become extinct over time, leaving only twitches in their place. He stands there, looking at them, as he is meant to. It is only because centuries separate him and them that they do not notice him.

A wind ripples Radha's yellow dupatta and the silver surface of the river bringing him back to movement. He turns away to the water. It is a narrow river. He can wade across it very easily. The nightglow makes the surface of the water shine, rendering everything below it opaque. He puts a foot into the water and the light breaks to make room for it and then the water closes again, and the light returns. Under his foot is the smoothness of stone. This forest began as a moment dilated. Now, he has traveled far, to its other edge.

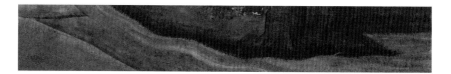

He wades across. There is a mango tree on the other side, from which fruit hang suspended in the darkness. As he puts his foot in the water he hears familiar laughter, and Tara appears from behind the trunk of the mango tree. She jumps up and down and laughs at the surprise in his eyes. She takes his hand and says, "I came to make sure you don't get lost. I'll take you as far as I can."

"Where are the storytellers?"

"They're still there, telling each other stories, they will go on for days."

"Will you tell me a story? About dawn at your home. I know very little about the dawn."

The traveler takes a deep breath.

"Already, while it is still dark, there is the sound of the washermen beating clothes on the stones at regular intervals, like a very loud heartbeat. As the light begins to appear, I can see from where I stand the washerman's cloth going up into the air before coming down hard on the stone again. The bell of the chapel rings and a few moments later the hymns begin. In the vacant patch of land next door, where six men look after piles of white marble and wood, one man shouts at his companions every morning. I don't know if it is the same discord that ruptures him everyday. I close the windows, and open them later, after he has stopped shouting—It's hard for me to describe these things."

The traveler becomes quiet, lost in what he has not said.

"It's enchanting. I would like to see it."

"Enchantment..."

"To hear or see what does not exist in your own world."

They both notice the light changing in the sky above them, the nightglow quietly easing its way out, and the beginnings of rising sunlight. They have left behind the river, the dark forest, and they have reached an open landscape of rounded hills and valleys.

"This is as far as I can take you, without getting lost myself." She smiles now, but there is a childlike regret in her dark eyes.

He goes down on his knees but cannot bring himself to hold her. They look at each other.

"Remember the necessity of opposites, the king and the sage, the night and the dawn, the grown up man and the little girl," she says.

Before he can reply she has turned around and is running, back towards the river, and the forest of trees.

He has no choice but to face the new landscape.

The green hills bear trees of darker green on the rims. The traveler feels his life can be saved, from the inside out. Between undulations there is a pond filled with lotus over which cranes are bending their necks. On the grass next to the pond lies a snake. Beyond the last undulation there hangs an immense sky, only beginning to be lit.

These are the landscapes he can walk through and go very far.

He thinks of a photograph he has seen of the earth taken from the gray surface of the moon. He is enchanted by that image too. When he looks at it the earth seems to be moving a little. But it cannot save his life, from the inside out. What is real then, and what is not?

C I T Y

THEY ROLL OVER and over on the ground, their long hair and already faded saris gathering soil and dust. Women not above forty, perhaps factory workers in the day, prostitutes at night, mothers in the twilight and early dawn. When their sari pallus fall away as they roll over and over, they reveal, under their blouses, the small bony mounds of their breasts.

A long road leads to the dargah. It begins with an enormous rubbish dump that seems to issue forth from the heart of the earth. It continues in craters of crushed stone gravel and black pebbles, along with large patches of melted tar. The May sun scorches everything in sight, including its own shadows. The road then turns left and narrows. There are shops on either side that sell withered roses, synthetic incense, and broken toys. Here the sun disappears completely, and takes the entire sky with it. Over this road there are rusted corrugated iron roofs, spreading wide. Underneath them, in spaces so compressed that a man can barely stand up, welding machines and lathes lie idle. Beneath this, the crowds press forward.

Sometimes, looking for a solitary dargah, a wanderer might unexpectedly find crowds celebrating the urs of the saint who lies buried there. Her body behaves differently than the crowds, standing very still when everyone else is restless, and impatient for movement when they are still.

The wanderer fears the equality that a crowd demands. People close in on all sides, pushing her along with an insistent hand on her back, colliding against her shoulder, her face. She sees herself as a solitary, though she may not be one. Suddenly, there is a hand, firm on her breast, squeezing and gone. She stops and turns around. But all she sees is men and women looking ahead of them. Someone says, "Keep moving!" and she's jolted forward.

The women who roll on the ground are not part of the moving crowd. They are separate, but the crowds make room for their separateness, just as they make room for an outsider. The women have come to ask of the pir who is buried here, the pir who will help them to become sane again. In a clearing a woman jerks her head down, and back up again. When the head goes down her long hair brushes the road, when she throws back her hair, it hits someone else's face like a whip. Sometimes, the women are accompanied by a sister, a friend, who offers them a glass of water, or steadies them with an outstretched arm. A woman dances to drumming, a dance of perfect wretchedness. The drums are without rhythm. They beat the closed, humid air into submission.

This crowd is not a river, flowing, or a forest, upward rising, or a field of wheat, open. It has no choice but to be a heap. It is composed of the most disparate things carelessly thrown in the same place—rituals, women in shine, men looking at the women, some felt faith. After they reach the dargah, they will once again know that what they wait for always disappoints, what comes unexpectedly may make a life turn.

The heap pushes itself onward. People urge each other ahead constantly, but with a calm impatience, as if impatience was not of the moment but a habit. They stop sometimes to watch the dancing women, without any emotion in their eyes. As they get closer to the narrow lane of the dargah, someone begins to caress her bare arm. The caressing continues for a few minutes till she is pushed forward by the crowd. What stays on her skin is not only the touch, but the force of a longing that cannot limit itself to the senses.

On this narrow, dark lane, in an empty space outside the dargah, under the leaden light which squeezes in from above, a young girl stands. She is still in her early teens, and wears a dress which may have been some other colour once, but is now only dirt brown. The dress falls away at both shoulders. The hushed crowd watches. The drummers stop playing. The crowd and the solitary suddenly coincide, they are both completely still.

The young girl spins slowly, with an ease supplied by tension, her left arm stretched out, the hand in a half fist as if grasping a pillar, but grasping only empty space. She spins around this absent pillar, creating a consummate silence. Outside it, there is the sound of metal being hammered on another street, and its long echo.

"Why are you here?" she asks the crowd, very softly, with resignation, as if any answer would be a lie.

The leaden light that falls on her is exactly the colour of the corrugated roofs, except with more luminosity, and it has the weightlessness of something that is free to pass over this street and never return.

"Go back, go back," she says, her voice becoming louder. "Go back to your kerosene stoves, to your factories, your festering babies."

The crowd watches.

"Go back to the nothing created for you in this filth."

People begin shifting and murmuring. She keeps spinning around nothing, an acrobat, a gymnast.

"Randi," someone says from the crowd. She raises her head and listens, in the direction of that word, carefully, as if listening to a fluteseller approaching from far away.

"Why are you here?" she says softly again.

"Go back to raping and being raped," she shouts. She takes her hands, utterly delicate and filthy, and covers the place between her legs. A grimace of pain crosses her face.

She leans now, with her left shoulder against the invisible pillar, and closes her eyes, perfectly balanced.

On either side of her, green, turbid water stands stagnant in the open drains. The smells of urine and excrement rise from them and merge.

Two men emerge from the crowd and knock her down. She falls slowly, without surprise. Another man emerges with the sacred broom from inside the dargah, otherwise used to bless worshippers. He beats her with the broom, and then hands the broom to one of the other men.

"Stop!" someone says from the crowd.

The men turn around as if at a slap.

"This is what she needs," they say. "This is what will cure her."

The girl begins to laugh, a woman's laugh and a child's together. The man beating her pulls away his stick in fright. Silence comes over the crowd again. The three men move away from her and watch her from a distance. The girl continues laughing. A small pool of blood collects around her pelvis.

An old woman in a burkha approaches the girl and showers rose petals on her. They are without fragrance, and so withered they look like bits of paper.

"Kill her," someone says.

A young woman begins to weep.

The one not part of this crowd, the traveler, the solitary, has some moments ago begun to push through the crowd, knocked about by shoulders and elbows and looks of surprise. When she reaches the girl and leans towards her, the girl whispers:

"Why are you here?"

————

THIS evening Gretta wears a black crocheted blouse, and the streetlamp lights up her face. It's Sunday and she's just returned from the church down the street where the sea begins, to her table covered with a flowered oilcloth set on the side of the street, where she sells cutlets made of mincemeat, or fish, or prawns. She wraps them carefully in butter paper and then a newspaper, making sure students and young people get a discount. Trucks, buses, water tankers splashing water behind them, motorcycles, cars, autorickshaws, and bullock carts go by on the street, so that sometimes she can't hear what the customer wants, or how many. This evening she invites a regular customer to come in and see her one room just off the deafening road, where she lives with her young daughter and her husband, who are not at home. She shows the visitor a room illuminated by two white lights that have neither shadows nor clarity. There is a gray formica table and three white plastic chairs, a bed with a gray and white bedcover, a refrigerator, a television, and a picture of Jesus with two unlit candles on either side. She doesn't show the visitor but the visitor notices the pea hen that stands on the bed. It has a tiny crested head, and a small neck made of an iridescent blue-green, the only real colour in the room. After the neck the body swells out in dull gray blue feathers. Sit down she says, while she herself keeps standing and begins to chop an enormous bunch of coriander leaves lying on the table. She asks the visitor that man who comes with you sometimes is he your husband, and when she hears yes, is he good to you, and seeing the visitor's smile she says you're fortunate. She says when I think of my childhood I feel such longing, such a pain in the centre of my chest, though she smiles as she says this and her dark eyes widen. Her body has been kneaded and softened by the years into middle age. She says, next to the church there were rice fields. They say it's good in Australia or New Zealand, she says, while the pea hen sits absolutely still on the bed, with its small crested head raised in alertness. I'm waiting to save enough she says, I own this room at least, I can sell it, but of course that won't be enough, will it, time, it'll take some time, but I have faith, you have to have faith. The pea hen emits a high pitched wail and flies up towards the ceiling, hovers for a moment and perches back on the bed again in complete stillness. The visitor's detailed, intricate education, and travel to far continents, and her understanding of the enquiry of different ages, suddenly begins to shrink, while Gretta's life grows larger. The visitor lets her small hands rest on her lap. Through the window she watches the smoke rise from the hundred year old chimney of the bakery next door. There are too many coriander leaves stuck to Gretta's fingers. She washes her hands in the ocean. Pray for me please, she says, and smiles. Waves drip from her palms. She dries them on a forest. The pea hen moves through the forest to where the peacock waits for her to open his fan. When evening comes, and she lights the two candles at her altar, the land glows and quivers all the way till the edge of the ocean.

A TAXI driver once asks her, "How long does it take to learn what you're learning?"

"At least ten or fifteen years," she says.

"Ten or fifteen years," he says, looking ahead at the unending traffic.

When she gets off, he says, "Let me do it."

He takes out the tanpura, slowly, diagonally, making sure it hits against nothing on either side, and puts it in her arms.

Once a week, she comes to learn this music. She eases her upper body in through the door of the cab and puts in the tanpura first, in its thick cotton cover, bending low and putting it diagonally across, the gourd on the back seat, the stem reaching past the side window in the front, then eases her body out, without hurting herself against the low roof of the cab, goes around to the other side and eases her body in again, sits down and puts an arm around the gourd to steady it, holding it constantly, awkwardly, on the forty minute ride.

There is no daylight here. In this small, carpeted, windowless room, the only light is the tiny yellow one directly above the framed image of Saraswati on the wall. Enormous trucks go by on the main road nearby, bringing goods from outside the city. Water tankers and long distance buses pass through. The stems of two tanpuras rise out of the darkness. At a few places their wood responds to the faint yellow light by gleaming, and the gleam moves as the body that holds the stem changes the rhythm of its breathing. Engines run loudly as they wait in the stalled traffic. When they move, gathering force and releasing even harsher sounds, their wheels break up the asphalt into craters, pebbles and gravel scatter in the air. She faces the young man her teacher. His family has played and sung this music for seventeen generations. The yellow light gleams also in the eyes, sometimes raised towards each other. As she begins, her voice falters, the note sustains for a few seconds, then breaks.

It is night in the forest.

In the foreground is the most reticent golden light, without any known source. It does not illuminate more than what is necessary, does not squander itself, is never more forceful than it needs to be. It is much more than a means to looking.

The light comes from within the darkness, as light often will. Then it matures into an extreme serenity. It may rise to create a nightglow in the sky, or remain close to the ground, on tree trunks and leaves.

Parrots fly through the trees. Akbar stands watching as Tansen sits before Swami Haridas. A sunflower on a long stem bends and hovers over him. Two banana trees spread their leaves on either side. Creepers fall to the ground through their branches. *Look, says the young man her teacher, how curious and skeptical Akbar's eyes as he looks at Swami Haridas.* As curious and skeptical as anyone looking at his own opposite. On the grass a peacock stands still. White flowers bloom on small bushes.

A little distance away from Akbar is Tansen, sitting with his legs folded behind him, looking at his guru. His face has the attention that an exacting reverence brings. A tanpura lies next to him on the grass. To the far right is Swami Haridas. *Tansen will have to travel the distance which is in Swami Haridas' eyes.* The Swami, still a young man, perhaps younger than Tansen, sits at the foot of a saptaparni tree. His bare body is almost skeletal, and he holds a tanpura in his right arm. He lets a thin branch of the tree pass over his arm, parallel to the stem of the tanpura. It erupts a little beyond his arm in a profusion of leaves.

The forest is conscious. Things curve and bend, but never droop. It is a place of rest, not languor. There are birds and flowers but not their extreme profusion. There is nothing in this forest that breaks the restraint of the universe.

What is a note? she asks.
Only a longing, he says.

68

Akbar stands erect, composed. He will not kneel or sit before Swami Haridas. Tansen sits as someone who has been changed by another, this man whom he faces. *He will always be in between.* Swami Haridas sits lightly on the grass. He will not stand up before the king. He is the only one whose arms are not close to the body but held away, the legs spread apart, one stretched out on the ground, the other bent at the knee and pulled upward, his person unguarded, open, susceptible to injury.

The colour of the light is the same as that of Swami Haridas' body. The light is as susceptible to being extinguished.

This light, she says. It can put her most vicious longings to rest. *I know, he says.* The space between Tansen and Swami Haridas is where the forest becomes inscrutable, made of impure black. *That is the way we have to walk, he says. Come.* Perhaps he thinks the light will become an undeserved solace if they stay too long, or that its extreme serenity will blunt the heart. But the light is percipient. Its serenity is for survivors. The light has learnt illumination from the sudden turnings of love, the dilemmas of the ascetic, and the movements of animals hiding from the arrow on night hunts.

She puts down the instrument and reaches across to touch her teacher's feet.

THE TANPURA sways on the back seat of the car, the gourd held by rolled up cloth on either side. She passes shut warehouses, a hardware shop ready to close, its fatigued white light illuminating the cobwebs in the back room while the hired boy sits beside his dreams in the darkness near the entrance, a nature park with its gate padlocked, large trees blackened by the night rising beyond it, till she stops at the traffic lights. A man in the car next to her turns his head and looks at her for a long time, a look so present, without past or future, that it untames time and throws it back into the wilderness from where it came. Teak trees fill the land, and the smaller cashew, with its ripening pink fruit, the road winds through them, far away the sky is held up by hills, and the world originates every moment. She turns her eyes away. In some years, when she is older, this look from a man will change. What is inevitable, like the future, comes in through the open windows and she breathes it in, isometrically, inspiration, expiration. Butterflies sleep in the nature park, the lights change. She drives on under a flyover where the darkness is thicker, almost hiding the mound of garbage piled up on one side, and then turns right onto the elevated highway where a radiant white light falls from the windows of enormous new office buildings made completely in glass. The tanpura suddenly gleams and shines. On either side and ahead are tall buildings still being built, with iron girders around them, sloping from the top down and wide at the bottom, with large, angled cubes as entrances, triangular or conical roofs, and cranes hang at the top of each one, lit by strong silver lights. The earth lights the sky instead of the sky the earth. In the racecourse stables, horses stand with their eyes open, silent. She goes under the new yellow skywalk hanging in the air, connecting the width of the highway, bright yellow even at night. A long time after the music lesson the sound of the tanpura remains around her, she can still hear its long, circular resonance. Only over a few hours will it completely fade away. At the red light a tall, muscular, large boned eunuch appears next to her window. His white teeth gleam in the darkness. "Such heavy thoughts," he says. He leans languidly against the car and puts out his large hand. She gives him a fifty rupee note. "You're beautiful," he says. "The fifty rupee note is beautiful," she says before driving on. The night is unreliable. Parallel to the road now are the train tracks and two trains go by in opposite directions. Exhaustion and energy change places continuously within the people inside, with no room or time for anything in between. White light spills out from the compartments, but it is not radiant like the light from the offices. This light is turbid and tough and accepting, it throws itself on to the sparse grass and rubbish that lines the tracks. Up on to another elevated highway, she drives faster, the air humid and cool through the windows, and the strings of the tanpura are played for a moment by the wind, producing a sound that is random, atonal, but still originary. It stops as the road slopes down, towards what looks from here like the edge of the earth, but is the sea, and after a long time, when her hair is tangled by the damp and soot in the air, the lights of the new cable stayed bridge over the sea appear, but which like this car, highways, skywalks, office buildings of glass, and train tracks, are the from elsewhere brought, because nothing rises here, like water, from far below, nothing begins or sprouts minutely as from a seed, or stirs, or raises its wings.

Under a raintree in the gardens of the irrelevant zoo, the white peacock opens its luminous ivory fan against the night.

The car moves on to the bridge. The water below is moving, but it cannot be seen, only a darkness is being crossed, the bridge and the sea are like a question and answer no longer related. When she reaches the end she turns left along the sea, on whose waters three ships, barely visible, like an unwanted past, are lined up in the far distance, there are still walkers on the promenade, there is the new concrete clock, shaped like a sickle which cuts the sea air in two. Along the promenade is the dense darkness of the mangroves. Unseen barnacles cling to the mesh of their roots. After that begins the transparent emptiness over the water. Where the mangroves end and the promenade crumbles into a broken footpath, there are fish drying on horizontal bamboo poles. What is new? Not that which is not old. In the time it takes to dry fish, the time that unfurls in the hawker's cry, in the time it takes to wear a sari, time is original, animate. Opposite the drying fish are the two-tiered shanties of fishermen and household workers. Their fronts are painted either the blue of the ocean on a clear, hot day, or the pink of sunrise, both exaggerated in their brightness. The resonance of the tanpura is further away now, receding but still present. She turns onto a side street past trees and apartments. The small Dalit shrine has an image of the Buddha, an oil lamp burning at his feet, the day's marigolds still fresh. Around the shrine the night is as tense as a fist. A little further is a remnant of the old village square, with a squat cross at its centre, an oil lamp burning at the foot of the cross, and on one side, two slumped cottages of wood and stone with no fight left in them. The night spreads out here, more malleable. Approach what is alive, go near, approach. Mourn that which is no longer living but should have been, mourn. Place what lives, next to one another, place, or watch them as they are placed, watch. Between them there are invisible joints that are uncertain, needing protection. Between them lies something dangerous, multiple fractures. Between them, the sight can see in every direction.

A few streets away from home now, past the closed tailor's shop, and suddenly there are ducks gathered under a streetlight. The night is disobedient. When she pulls up she sees them standing there, hovering over a puddle of dark water in a small crater made by broken paving stones. There are seven of them, tall and snow white, untouched by the soot and grime in the air, with bright orange beaks and feet. She stops the car and turns off the lights. Their bodies tremble, then hold absolutely still. They all crowd around, one by one, to look at her. They hold still, but their breath is animal breath, visible in the swell and fall of their bodies, tangible, crucial. One of them comes up to the window, and holds its face close in front of hers. The streetlight glints off the black marble of its eye. The gaze between it and the dark pupil of her own eye is the gaze between two distant stars.

When she reaches her street there are no lights on it, no lights in the entire neighbourhood. The power failure allows the street to be filled with leaf shadows, mango, coconut, jamun, fishtail palm, the leaves of one tree touching another on the concrete paving blocks. The almost full moon is directly overhead. She carries the tanpura up the unprepared darkness of the stairs to the third floor and stands it up near the bookshelves. Where she goes to learn this music there are no bookshelves, no books. Outside the window, fruit and bats hang from the tamarind tree. Each leaf of each tree is illuminated or not by chance, a silver leaf moving next to one that is dark, but both wakeful, conscious of each other. The breeze brings the rise and fall of human voices, in a lower key, each one attuned to this night. In the plot of land used as a storage ground, piles of white marble shine.

Beyond it the white chapel on a rising slope from 1856, the time of the Portuguese fathers, working among rice fields and fishing boats, claims the moonlight as its own. Next to it the old mansion of wood and stone stands, self assured, receives the light on its roof of Mangalore tiles, then passes it down to the balconies, the trees, and shrubs close to the ground. Night, wide open, is here, made from primary principles, woven into a Bengal neelambari sari deep blue and filled with stars, painted for centuries as night of love never night of fear, never, night of Radha and Krishna where nothing will be excluded, neither forest, nor animal, nor human, neither here nor there, night indistinguishable from Kali who appears after all the flames and the philosophies, after the mourners have brought down the flaming sticks on the ones they loved and walked away without looking back, night staying awake outside a semi-circle of caves after the fire has burnt to ashes, night that the ascetic questions, night from which anything can be built, she leans on the silver light, night of the declining heart, therefore night of ascesis, capable of freeing itself from all contexts, original.

Throughout this night, the street shows its age. It is mature, like all things that bear. It has been able to think a thought through over lifetimes.

———
THE refrigerator was as old as the building being repaired, more than fifty. It was stolen by the repairmen when they were repairing his building. He is seventy seven and lives alone on his pension. They say his brothers swindled him, left him nothing from his inheritance. He used to work in a bank. He knows everything about being practical but has no desire to put that knowledge to use. Every morning he goes to the Irani. He orders three cups of tea, all at the same time, and one brun. He borrows the day's newspaper from the owner, a man in his fifties. He reads it as he has his tea and brun. He knows the news of the world. He knows the rise and fall of the stockmarket. He rarely speaks to anyone. Once he didn't come for a long

time. The waiters were worried, and the owner. When he came in after a month he said he'd been very ill, with jaundice. But he wasn't afraid at all, he told them. He knew he wasn't going to die. He knows when he will die, he is clairvoyant. He tells them the date and the year. He writes it down on a piece of paper. On the way out he greets the owner sitting at his counter, reading a book. In the evening he returns and buys—at a reduced price— the newspaper that he has already read that morning. The owner offers to give it to him, but the man insists on paying for it. Some days, when he walks out with the paper, he looks up at the sky. On the street, buses, trucks, bicycles, iron carts and cars go by. He looks up and sees a full moon. People walk by and around, he gets brushed against, pushed, elbowed. But nothing can move him. His tall, thin body which always seems to have too many bones, and trembles a little at all times, suddenly becomes as still and firm as a mountain. He stands there and keeps looking. He keeps looking up at the moon.

Old mirrors line one wall inside, made of thick glass, an image of Zoroaster at the centre. Black spots and smears bloom through the glass in places. White light falls from the high ceiling, the same dull cloudy light of other shops and homes where bank notes are always counted out with great care, or anxiety, or sadness. But here, the mirrors impart a glow, however redundant. The cook stands in his undershirt at the back near the blackened kettles and pans. He makes the flexible tea which, at the old marble topped tables, is a way of silence or the rest in conversations, or conversely its source of energy, with or without milk, with or without sugar, with or without lemon, but boiled till only a crucial robustness remains. A man leans against the counter as he waits for his bread, taking a break from impatience. The one who watches sees all of this leavened, by his own gaze, into a patient, grimy beauty.

The owner looks up from his book and sees the old man looking at the moon.
This place has been left to him by his father.
You ask why I've settled in these emerald mountains

His father never sat here with a book.

and so I smile, mind at ease of itself, and say nothing.

He didn't know how to read.

Peach blossoms drift streamwater away deep in mystery:

It's another heaven and earth, nowhere among people.

"I don't know what I would do if I went in to the middle of nature," he says. "I don't think I would know what to do. But show me any writing as beautiful as Li Po's. Any poets like Du Fu or Wang Wei."

———

JARI MARI MATA is a face carved in silver, set on curving stone that has been painted a bright orange, a face of peace and attention, the eyebrows raised slightly in quiet concern, almond shaped eyes, the nose slim and perfect, the full lips brought together in the beginnings of a smile. There is a long line throughout the day to make an offering before her. The temple opens early and closes late. The flowers—lotus, marigold, red hibiscus, jasmine—accumulate in two small mounds on either side of her face. At times the line is slowed down by someone in insurmountable grief, or with a problem as complex as fate.

The pujari is always patient, always generous. He listens to the problems of the worshippers. Here, only the poor have something to tell him. He knows, like him, they have nowhere else to go. The ones who drive up in cars, men and women, make their offerings without saying a word.

Late at night, after the temple doors that open directly onto a main avenue are closed, the pujari gathers up all the flowers that have been offered to the Mata. He puts them in an enormous bag. He steps out and empties it into a large pond across. On the avenue women and eunuchs blossom. He indicates to one of the women, dressed in tinsel and dark pink, that he will be out soon.

Inside, he removes the silver face of the goddess. He pulls it off in one strong upward motion. Below it is the original face in stone, painted orange. The eyes here are two enormous white circles with the lower corners pointing downwards, the large pupils painted black, the nose smashed flat and set somewhat askew, the lipless mouth as wide and exaggerated as that of a large fish, held open, offering a deep, dark space inside. There is nothing to indicate whether the face is a woman's or a man's.

The pujari cleans the silver face with a damp cloth, and leaves it lying on one side. Then he cleans the face of orange stone. He says his own prayers, to the unmasked god, locks the doors and emerges on the avenue.

––––

THE mochi is inside his wooden box, made to the height and width of him sitting cross-legged. His knees rest on a narrow ledge outside the box, amidst broken shoes, hammers, cans of glue, nails and an anvil. In the few inches of space behind him, within the box, he hangs the shoes that he has finished working on. Above this he keeps the smallest altar with faded pictures of the Devi riding a tiger, and Jesus, and a saint with a turban, and the Buddha smiling his translucent smile, and Ambedkar. The mochi is in the sky. The box, painted a blue lighter than this sky, rides the wind. A gigantic eagle hovers above and casts the shadow of its wings on the surface of the ocean. He perches on the mochi's box without weighing it down. He moves his wings, stroking the waves without touching them. The sun is about to set, its last light behind gathered clouds. My doctor says, now look down at the earth from very far above. Yes. Your life is a line of light inside a transparent, thin cylinder stretched out on the ground, over a vast distance. Do you see it? Yes. I see the line on the earth, next to the ocean. But there is no light in it, except very far away, towards the future. The universe is very old, says the doctor. I see only what I move towards, I tell him, not what I have been or what I now am. I pay attention to the past and the present only because they lead to what will come. The mochi lights a candle at his altar. It brings the dimmest glow to the chest of the eagle above, and to a shard of the water below. He stitches a sole on a shoe, lifting the large, thick needle high into the evening. Pin pricks of blood appear in the sky, like the last residues of sunset. The mochi, for a moment, looks out over the ocean. Only what is continuous, what is unbroken, gives rest. The eagle folds his wings. He comes from a high wilderness, from a place without dust, where the earth has not been broken open. He can see very far, to where the rabbit, his prey, moves under bushes two miles away, and right through to the other side of the human heart. The mochi and I face each other, as we have done for eleven years. My black, high heeled shoes lie on their side on his ledge. One of the heels is broken. I haven't finished yet, he says, glancing at them. You had asked me to soften the edges of the two straps so they don't cut the skin on your feet. That takes time. I can wait, I say. So dark, he says, isn't it, a moonless night. Do you remember, he says, there were two full moons last month. The doctor's voice rises and falls now, like a hawker walking down a long street. The universe has its own answers, he says. If you go into this ocean below, diving under water, with a ship coming in to anchor, you will go next to the quiet authority of the ship, through the frailest plants with leaves as thin as hair being swayed by the water exactly like a plant swayed by the wind above, over stones that may have come to rest on the seabed that very day or a century ago, through schools of small black fish, or a single orange one alone, the seabed itself gradually being extended by volcanic eruptions, as you probably know, that harden into a crust. The oldest rocks on the bottom of the ocean are approximately two hundred million years old. The doctor knows that only what is continuous, what is unbroken brings rest. But for how long? He takes a handkerchief and brings it down on my tears. He is tender but careful, he does not touch my skin even once. The saint at the mochi's altar would have used his bare hands. The eagle sits still on the box. His large pupils have taken in the gleam of the earth with minimal diffraction. He has passed it through his body. He has not finished considering it. He moves to the edge of the box, leans forward, and raises his enormous wings. The mochi looks up and sees him for the first time. A tear drops from his eye. This eagle is from outside time, like the human stain that nothing can cleanse, neither birth nor death nor life, nor rebirth. The eagle has seen the doctor and the mochi, both trying to make unbroken what is broken, endless work. He has seen the line of my life far below on which the mochi's candle now casts a distant glow, and far beyond that, to those interstices of the earth where ascesis and instinct are as one. He rises into the air slowly but there is urgency in the beating of his wings. Time is infinite but never enough. The eagle's attributes are his tools, the panoramic image on his retina, the manifold sounds in his ear. With these he gathers pieces of consciousness from which he will build his eyrie, high above the earth but unmistakably on it. The pills the doctor finally has to prescribe are to be taken thrice a day, called Stablon, they are small, smooth, brilliant white, and swollen in the middle, holding the chemical tianeptine, first synthesized by French researchers Antoine Deslandes and Michael Spedding in the early eighties. It is known to be effective much of the time, but it is not known yet exactly why. The research into human misery, they say, has barely begun. But the homeostatic mechanisms of unhappiness bequeathed by evolution can be dismantled and replaced as research grows. What is stable is what holds together, able to bear every centrifugal force, unlike myself. The eagle flies towards land, gripping the sky with his talons, over dark holes gaping from earth, baring iron teeth. He leaves behind a diurnal awareness. The box shakes as the eagle flies away and a hammer falls from the mochi's ledge, like a dislodged mountain rock. Everything is precarious, everything hangs on nothing. The night takes the hammer's falling force, its surface swells with a bruise. "Come by tomorrow evening then," the mochi says. He doesn't say this is all I can ever do, make sure that your shoes don't bruise your feet, and I don't say my feet are always bruised, and they are unsteady, and I often stumble and fall, and he doesn't say I don't have time to look up, like everyone who hammers, sews, ploughs, digs, weaves, grinds, and gathers, and I don't say I am too much looking up, looking skywards, and we live every day despite the facts that make us, despite the hands that serve feet, and my own hands that do not ever shake, but are excessively at rest.

―――

IT IS July and the rains have gathered force, coming down hard on roads and rooftops and swaying trees; it turns dark at six in the evening, not yet the time for twilight in this season, and there is the call of the vegetable seller who arrives always at six, exactly, no matter what the weather; today he is wearing a transparent hooded raincoat and the vegetables on his cart are covered with a thick blue sheet of plastic, the blue that the sky will be after the monsoons have gone; the rain is all around him, over him, the rain wetting his face, his trousers and his feet; and it would be hard even to keep one's eyes open standing in that rain, and there seems no reason to stand there because not a single person is on the street today as he calls, throwing his voice as loudly as he can so that he can be heard above this downpour; a young man using his skill in pitch and tone to throw his voice above the bass, flat sound of the rain, as the street darkens even more, and no one appears, and in his call there comes, very slowly, a higher pitch, and he is no longer calling but demanding; in response the rain falls even harder; he answers by raising both volume and pitch, and this forces him to open his mouth wider, and bare his teeth, and approach the beginning of anger.

―――

SILVER mackerel and pink ladyfish wait on broken plywood boards at the end of the street, with the patience that comes only after death, to be sold by large, strong boned women squatting below yellow streetlamps. A wide and tenacious pelvis centres their bodies as they squat, bend and lift. In the long wait between customers, they bargain silently with the night. Mother Mary in the small shrine next to them has been made in their image, as large and strong, even corpulent, dressed in a blue sari with golden stars and a little golden crown. Opposite the shrine a thin old woman hangs from the concrete lattice work of the dargah with her back to the street, trembling all over, shaking the night at its edges.

Emptiness is long enough for a whole street to enter. It is high enough to reach the troposphere, and from there the stars that are able to shine only in a clear winter sky like this one. They shine down on the star anise below, lying open on a wooden spice cart, next to the cardamom, cinnamon, bay leaves and pepper. What grows from the earth and what grows from the sky can be shaped exactly like each other. The seller of spices looks at the sky as he looks at the blackened wall across the street. He asks her, what would you like to buy, and she says, no I'm traveling soon, and he asks where to, Switzerland? as if he, who has been nowhere, had seen Zurich in her eyes, and she, surprised, says yes, but when I'm back home I'll buy from you. The butcher brings down his broad, flat knife through the conversation, and splits the skin and muscles of a goat. He hangs up the different parts on hooks above him and then sits between them, his knife silent in his hands.

The thing about emptiness is that it is wide enough to stretch sideways to the ocean just behind these houses, where used plastic bags and decomposing waste pretend to be sand, and after that to the water, and finally the clean, clear rim of the horizon. People go away to Canada and Australia, leaving the fishing to the large trawlers, abandoning wooden homes whose carved balconies and sloping roofs from the last century are now collapsed, becoming dark matter occupying space, humus, essential to the fertility of this earth.

The young tailor finishes measuring the back of the young woman who smiles at the street while being measured, and then carefully takes the smile away before turning back. The two young men who work at the new Chinese restaurant exactly opposite the tailor take her smile and keep it safely, to use at a later time. They watch the foreigners who have arrived from very far away to live on this street, from the same lands to which people from here have gone to live a better life. The foreigners never come to the new restaurant, but stand on the street and eat the rounds of vegetables fried before them, satisfying a hunger that has been inside them since they were born.

Emptiness has returned here over and over to be filled. There is no less truth in this than in those who live and sell on this street, no more truth in that which stays than that which passes through. Often, that which passes through is a funeral procession with a brass band.

———

"SEVEN hundred years ago when this was built," says the dargah keeper, "there were forests here." He sits on the verandah of the small dargah all day, with three other men, and looks out at the forest of the four lane arterial road that cuts the through the middle of the city. They have sat here for decades, their sitting without season, their eyes still and the gaze very far, towards horizons in forest clearings. Birds rise from them and return. The trees are always ripe, the fruit rising, the leaves stretching outwards. Time is so large that the present can be easily overlooked. Inside the room with the tomb, a man kneels and prays. The dargah keeper repeats himself, "Seven hundred years," he says again and again to the traveler. He keeps on answering a question that was asked only once, replying to the many times that no one has asked it. "Older than old," he says. The traveler walks around the shrine. He looks in through a window, and sees the man inside continuing to pray, with his eyes closed, his palms raised to his chest, side by side. Behind the man a gold cloth hangs on the wall. This is not a gold with which idols are adorned, not the gold which is now on women's clothes and shoes, not the gold worn by brides and grooms. This is a kneeling gold, certain of itself, but held in the cloth, needing to be found, and when found, a luminous indication that there will always be something in belief that there will never be in doubt, regardless of the newest art, or the finding of far planets. The old men sit with their hands resting on the edge of the verandah. What they hear is the azan rising from the great mosque on the next street, the ships coming in from the fifteenth century bearing surma, saffron and sufis, and the waves breaking on the other shore of the Arabian Sea.

THE ghada, the matka, the kolsi, made of clay, is perhaps the oldest way of storing water. It had to be tipped forward for the water to flow out. The water was cool on a burning day, and sweet, and it had the fragrance of clay, water from earth. A young boy might have gone from street to quiet street on the hottest afternoon, with the ghadas piled on a donkey's back, selling to the homes on either side. Now, the ghada is banished to the far edges of cities, small towns. It may be found in a mosque in the wilderness. The young man, her music teacher, says, "My father used to tell me, remember the ghada. It has been fired and can never be remolded, it can only break."

When an object sets, the metaphor that came from it is the light it leaves behind. To surrender to the fire in which it is shaped, afterwards never to give in, but always able to contain. In the universe of every extinct object, its implications are in orbit. Not in the objective light of museums, but in the darkness of individual memories.

The music teacher says, "The past can be loved, the future can only be anticipated. The past is made of matter, the future is empty space."

WHEN the traveler is at home, she is always and only at home. Milk is boiled every day. On copper water jars, bell metal plates, and old silver glasses, eruptions of darkness appear. There is no such thing as still life. The difference between light and shade has reached its culmination. The entrance to a cave is dark, and above, an entire sky burnt white by the sun. Outside the door, on the staircase landing, a fish in a palm comes forth from the daytime darkness, two arms holding ironed clothes, a green coconut, a nose ring, each lit only by its own origin. It is not only her own pupils that dilate when she watches. What is looked at grows large. Inside, water taps swell and bamboo blinds expand, wood stretches. Nothing contracts except untouched fruit in a bowl. When the eyes come back from watching, the pupils have moved that imperceptible distance in, towards the central axis of the body, the eyelids lowered. The eyes of the Bodhisatva Padmapani have returned from the scorched world of light outside the cave, and the world of dark shadows inside where both jewels and sweat gleam, he has drunk the dark water in the silver glass. Too much has passed for the face to be anything but still, otherwise it could not remain a face.

Into the stone courtyard, the sun falls without a single interruption at noon. Inside the cave, only two stone feet, one crossed over the other. Meanings change as the sun moves, they contradict each other, are ploughed and overturned with the seasons. Light cleaves the surface of human intentions. At twilight, a shoulder, on which the evening will rest.

When the day is finally curving over into evening, the vermillion gulmohur attains its colour, it rises from the darkness of its own leaves. Below it the hawker makes his last cry, and only the white vegetables on his cart can still be seen. His cry is not a string of words but an abstraction of sound because even what is most real must sometime be free of its reality, and the airplane flies on its everyday path exactly above the hawker, and the Bodhisatva Padmapani hears the birds returning, all the hundred and forty seven species that live above the ravine. Inside the home light is pulling away from stone, wood, copper, brass, glass, paper, steel. The koel calls in the tree, opening its beak and filling the sky with its voice, and then sits absolutely still. The Bodhisatva Padmapani looks at it once, momentarily raising his lowered eyelids. Now the gulmohur has become only points of light in the near darkness. She walks backwards in to the centre of the home, which is to say herself, never turning her face away from the darkening light, walking in, one step behind the other. When she looks up a few windows outside are lit from within with a golden light, and unexpected corners in her room glow, high up, unreachable, like parts of her life. The Bodhisatva puts down the lotus in his hand, and regards the flame that has been lit in the oil lamp, and his already still mind slowly becomes like the flame that does not flicker even once, behind his downward gaze the force of the basalt that he rests on, the lava that made the basalt, the volcano from which the lava erupted, the tectonic plates that pulled apart and the plates that converged to make the volcano, the force of a being who has watched the light and shadow move over everything, and only then turned his eyes away.

When incisions have been made in the basalt with hammer and chisel, wooden sticks or bamboo are inserted in them, and the incisions then flooded with water. The Bodhisatva waits for the rock to crack and give way. It will crack before his patience does. Then they will break the flank of the hillside, and excavate it for prayer and shelter.

On the trade routes nearby, muslin and spices and lapis are in movement, coming to rest at evening marketplaces along the way. When she does leave the house after dark, only for what is necessary, the market is swollen with fruit, and vegetables and flowers, wheat being ground, garlands being strung, cobblers and tailors stitching, flies suspended over sweets in glass cases. The evening is filled with the blunted despair of buyers, and the sharp relief of the sellers, hands giving and taking, money counted, the gaze always near, minute, required, everything illuminated.

She returns from the market to the darkness of her home. The light from the small street, the buildings outside, a round lamp above a gate, are enough to see by. These lights dimly illuminate the outward curve of a copper pitcher, throw shadows of the bamboo blinds on the wall, every thin horizontal strip of bamboo precisely drawn. That heaviness on the left is a cupboard, Burma teak become one with the darkness. Books are dark behind the darkened glass shelves, and in a black and white photograph there shines only the white winter sky of a foreign country. In the dark, objects assume more than their function. The contact of matter with light and season and human life is intricate and unpredictable. In the darkness objects reveal their ethics. They reveal everything they live by. Slowly the self, tired of so much consolidation, can stretch, even disperse, into the things that surround it. She feels the concrete awning over the large, open windows as some larger protection, like a father long gone. Human hands make more than what they know. In this darkness she can see the Bodhisa-tva more clearly. He moves away from all the oil lamps that have been lit inside the caves, and steps out under the night sky.

CAVES

THE BODHISATVA Padmapani has his eyes turned away.

The crowds swell in this large cave, pushing each other past frescoes of palaces, kings, princesses, trees and birds. Outside, the monsoon rain falls without a break, changing only from heavy to light and back again. The monks would have been in their monsoon retreat at this time, in one place from June to September, not resuming their wandering lives through fields and villages till the rains were over. White water rushes through a gorge below. There is a long gray patch over the right eye of the Bodhisatva, like an oversized, displaced tear. In front of him a sudden stillness comes over the crowds. For a very few, brief moments they stand quietly looking at the Bodhisatva, with the world behind him, even the lotus unregarded in his hand. The natural cunning of the soul at once recognises the power of the Padmapani. It makes people turn their backs even as they continue to face what they see. There is blue on the tips of the lotus petals, and in the centre of the necklace—lapis. It came from the mines of Badakshan in Afghanistan, to this solitary place close to the routes of trade, in the fourth or fifth century. The blue of the lapis takes the eyes inward, unlike the reds and browns that surround it. The painters used it sparingly, perhaps as a consequence of what they saw in the land, the scarp of Ajanta brown and gray, with scrub and rust red soil. Only rarely a small lake, stunned by the dry heat, or a withered pond. The turned away crowd turns away.

The headdress, the eyes, the lapis centre of the necklace and the lotus form the main axis of sight. There are affinities between them, and contradictions, that like the sight, dilate and contract. An awareness of this remains in the turned away eyes of the Bodhisatva as his gaze travels left and downwards, without conclusions.

A group of boys in their teens arrives before the Padmapani. They too become still for a while, and then as if shaking off a brief affliction they begin to move and laugh. They nudge one another. One of them slips under
the rope that cordons off the paintings. He stands with his back to the
Padmapani and strikes a pose almost identical to the one on the wall. His
young body seems to have its own knowledge, preserved through centuries, of how to bend the torso, to tilt the head. Then he turns his eyes away
exactly like the Bodhisatva. The crowd that has just arrived holds its breath
in surprise. The boy holds the pose for a few minutes, steadily. The crowds

keep watching. It is the boy who begins to laugh suddenly and the crowd laughs too. The laughter echoes in the damp, dark cave. When the boy slips back under the rope and straightens up, our eyes suddenly meet.

I move away to one side of the cave, waiting for the crowds to thin a little. Stefan remains standing there, watching. Small white lights at waist level illuminate the paintings. The crowds move so rapidly through the cave and out that it seems as if it is the princesses on the wall with their jewels, and the birds and monkeys on the trees that are watching the crowds with a surprised stillness. When we move out to the arched entrance of the cave we find rain pouring on the black stone stairs and filling the empty space above the gorge. We stand there watching the rain, huddled among the shouting crowds. The way we look at the rain is the way we looked at the Bodhisatva Padmapani, continuously. When we go back inside to wait till the rain eases, our eyes have to adjust again to the sudden darkness.

"Look," says Stefan. He takes my hand and guides me to a stone pillar. On the high bracket of this pillar are lovers, tilted out and downwards, as if in flight. Our hands remain together. We watch with our faces raised up. We follow these arms which hold, these legs which fold and rest, to their very end, till we stand close to the place from where they have come. The lovers are reminders, confirmations, that whatever seems awkward in a gesture can have as its source the most fecund of emotions, the foremost among them being love.

The boys are behind us, watching the sculpted couple, watching us. They seem less restless, more tense, more focused. They look at Stefan, wondering perhaps at the difference in our ages, Stefan almost sixty and myself a year away from forty. The difference seems greater, perhaps, because I look a few years younger than I actually am. The boys scrutinize me. While I try to keep my eyes on the sculpted couple I see that the couple is neither young nor old. When we leave, the boys follow us outside. The rain is still falling heavily, so we sit on the landing of the cave, just outside the reach of the rain. The boys stand on the other side of the entrance, to our left, and light up cigarettes. They laugh and yell, looking at us every few minutes. Finally they decide to leave, screaming, singing loudly and soaking themselves in the pouring rain.

The gorge here is semi circular. At the centre of it a stream springs from its source, flowing downwards in a series of waterfalls. In its flow it carves out seven bowls of rock which form small lakes. The water falls to the bottom of the gorge and becomes a river. When the rain stops people gather here at the river's edge. They eat bhajias fried in a huge kadahi, drink bottled cold drinks, laughing and shouting. A radio plays film songs. Young and middle aged men leer at all women except the very old. They spread out over the rocks by the river and one or two take off their shirts and jump into the shallow pool at the end of the stream, evoking more shouts and laughter. The water comes down with such force from the height of the cliffs that it is foaming white in the river. It takes with it rocks, plastic bags with bits of food inside them, pebbles, clumps of hair, bottle caps, leaves, a used sanitary napkin, a crushed feeding bottle.

"I'm the foreigner but it's you that everyone keeps looking at," says Stefan, smiling. I look around to see a group of women in bright saris and glass bangles staring at me. I let them be and look at the river running in the gorge, and the massive wall of the scarp across. I want only to be in this place and with this man I have met ten days ago. The sun comes out suddenly. It clarifies the shadows and rough wrinkles under Stefan's eyes, and the skin, a little swollen all over. He touches my face for the first time, with the tips of his fingers. We look at each other. The look has barely begun to travel and search when a shadow falls on us. It is the boys, bare bodied, in a circle, five of them, looking at us. Stefan takes his hand away.

Their bodies are, without exception, thin and bony, the chests concave. Only the colour of the skin varies from one to the other. I avoid looking at their faces.
"What's your name?" Stefan asks the one closest to us.
There is no reply. They keep looking at us.
"I think we," I say.
"No. We should stay." Stefan continues to look at them without moving. One of the boys, smaller than the others, makes a gesture, and they leave, though turning back several times to look at us. They move a short distance away to where their shirts are spread out to dry on the rocks. They jump from one sharp rock to another. One of them does somersaults.

THE traveler is unfinished.

He hovers over gorges. He looks up at open skies. No airplanes, no steel, no white lights, no huddled griefs in carpeted, windowless spaces. He is on a western shore of the subcontinent. The coastline is made of the darkest rocks. *These rocks were part of Gondwanaland, before the continents drifted apart. They say now that the earth's crust does not move continuously, that it stops sometimes, pauses and begins again. They say the Pacific Ocean is slowly, slowly closing, as the Atlantic opens.* He moves over the always maturing earth, through winding roads past cashew and breadfruit and mango trees, the mango beginning to flower in pale, greenish yellow spikes. The road winds up and down, comes out onto flat land with rocks and red soil, then begins to wind again towards the coast. *This land is the oldest and most stable in the subcontinent.* His anxieties appear suddenly and a grief that seems to have no source. They come perhaps from somewhere outside his life, preceding it. There is nothing, says his mind, where he is going, he should turn back. But he keeps traveling as if he and his mind were not one. He reaches a cape at noon and looks down from a promontory at the ocean just below, deep blue and shored with palms, *the Indian Ocean is the calmest ocean,* the waves, from up here, breaking soundlessly at the bottom of the trees, *the Indian Ocean is the warmest ocean,* on the hill the ruined walls of an old fort, a cannon, exactly the colour of the dark rocks, over which weeds and plants have grown, a small chapel built of mud and wood and sun and shadow, in which three children sit, watching their mother kneel in prayer, over everything the alert, dilated silence of land's end. His anxieties leave him slowly, for now.

Because his fears travel with him, he knows also the complete reality of their leaving. He watches how they leave when he feels within himself a movement towards something, a cape, a woman kneeling. Travel imitates this movement but only sometimes becomes it.

THERE are caves with innumerable pillars, each one differently carved. The pillars grind the sunlight that comes in from the entrance into a dark illumination. They end high up in brackets of lovers. Above the lovers, painted on the ceiling, are white flowers and leaves and birds on dark black. We move through a whole cave, looking up, a posture from the time of open skies. The oldest places require the oldest gestures, the least under human control, looking upwards always towards something larger, something that cannot be touched with the hands. The boys have followed us in. They are still bare bodied, with their shirts tied around their hips. They never look up. They lean against the pillars and smoke, flicking ash on the ground. To them, everything here seems to be bare rock and stone, even the sculpted lovers, numerous, on the top of every pillar, which they only glance at briefly. One of them lies down on the cool stone ground, and stretches. They have a sense of abandon that comes from not being watched by people they have known all their lives, the privacy that an unknown place brings. Perhaps this is what unites them to myself and Stefan. One of them lets out a long howl that echoes incessantly. For a moment I understand them.

The caves often have an upper storey with a small arched window carved in the centre. Inside one cave we find steep steps going up, but with a locked wooden door at the end. Stefan finds the caretaker who says he must go to the main office and get a key. He returns after a long time. He is a tall lanky man in his sixties. When he sees me he stops to look, lingering on every part of my body. Stefan holds my hand all the way up the stairs. Wherever we are his body always turns in my direction, unobtrusively, as if to include mine. I don't know if my body responds in the same way. The caretaker keeps turning back to look at us, especially at our joined hands.

The ceiling is very low up here, just high enough for a man to stand up. There is a small alcove in one wall. Stefan walks to the window and bends down to look outside. There are no paintings here, no ornamentation, and the light is like darkened silver. This is the season when the monks would have spent the most time in these caves, reading the scriptures, eating, meditating, being still. This was the one season when they did not move, could not move. Outside, clouds covered and uncovered the sky, the rain fell, the river ran in the gorge, insects and snakes emerged from the depths of the soil, plants rose high and spread further their leaves. They would have watched the outside, watched themselves.

"There is something unfinished..." says Stefan, speaking partly to himself. "Here. Something without conclusions."

In this gray, empty cave, time assumes its rightful dimensions. There is nothing here to distil it into eternity. The poise of thousands of years is different from a few hundred. Hills are hacked into caves, trade routes change their course like rivers, and what people learn covers over what they used to know, like a new continent covering a sea, for the mind is finite like the earth, these caves are abandoned, left to animals and birds who are equally, the Buddha said, Bodhisatvas, and so many centuries pass in this way that when a new, focused human gaze finds them again, they are still living so far within themselves that it is no longer possible to reach them. Time here has a raw, muscular poise, it is original, it will not back away, especially before those who have seen everything and know everything, and who can even tell what the future will bring.

"I know why you brought me here," says Stefan.

The boys are climbing up the stairs. Too soon, they reach the upper storey. The dark silver light turns heavy and leaden as it touches them. In the grayness their faces seem more manifest, their bodies become individual. I notice stone hard collarbones, enormous ears, sunken bellies, crooked necks. They seem to belong in this light, which now begins to resemble the hopeless twilight of forgotten towns to which they will have to return. There, a life's expectations crowd together and wait as evening comes over a main street of layered dust and tin-roofed shops, and insects revolve under the arc of weak willed streetlamps. All day they stand around in groups, laughing, sometimes pushing one another in jest. But it is now that the waiting becomes filled with tension, and a film song on the radio, even an unexpected wind, promises the unimaginable new. But nothing arrives except the night. The energy inside them decomposes, leaks, and sticks to anything it touches.

I look for the first time at their faces. One has a sadness so recessed that its reason will never be found. And one an excitement that fears the quiet. And then I notice that two of them are carrying large cricket bats. Closest to me is a face so distanced from everything that nothing can travel inwards, food but not nourishment, light but not the ability to see.

"What?" I ask them.

"Nothing," one of them replies. "Nothing," says another.

Stefan turns and sees the boys.

"Let's," I say to Stefan.

We begin to walk towards the steps.

The boys surround us.

"Why have you come to this place?" asks the boldest one, who seems to be their leader.

"To... see the Bodhisatva Padmapani."

"That effeminate man holding a flower in his hand, that old, faded painting?"

"It's beautiful."

"Beauty..." His eyes wander, and come to rest on the opposite wall. He seems to lose himself in a thought he cannot quite grasp.

I wish there was something on the walls, the wing of a bird or the shoulder of a man, however faded. It might have saved us.

"I think," Stefan says and he takes my hand.

The boys step closer and block our way. They separate my hand from Stefan's.

"Why are *you* here?" I ask.

"To spit on the Bodhisatvas," he laughs. He throws out a ball of spit which arcs across and lands next to me. He puts his hands on his hips. "And to look at people like you."

He slaps Stefan across the face. Stefan steadies himself. I can see he is trying not to respond.

One of the boys asks me, "Why are you with him?" It is not a question. They all stand firmly rooted now, looking at me as if they had a right to be answered.

I have nowhere to put my hands, so I cross my arms and hold myself. It's the wrong move.

They step forward and push me down to the ground. They pull Stefan away from me.

"We are not paintings and sculptures, we are real."

They rip off the front of my shirt. I can see the end of a bat coming at me and I try to move but it lands hard on my right shoulder, and the upper part of my chest. The pain takes away my sight for a moment. When I open my eyes again, I see one of the boys bringing his mouth to my bared breast. I feel his cold mouth and even colder saliva. I push with an immense hatred and fear. I see the thin boy flung against the hard stone wall. Then I fall.

I close my eyes. When I open them again I know the boys are there, shouting amongst themselves but I no longer see them. I see the caretaker looking at me and smiling, almost happy.

I close my eyes. When I am able to open them again I see from where I am, out through the small window, outside my life, a waterfall running down to the gorge below.

I close my eyes. I open them again and the cave is silent, there seems to be no one there. But in a corner I see a monk, wearing a dark red robe the colour of my blood, reading by the light of a trembling candle. I can see the curled edges of the papers he holds, his rough brown hands, his bent head. The candle has burnt down almost to the end, and he lights another, long and new, and steadies it next to the old one. It is dark night, and there is the sound of falling rain outside. The monk raises his face.

I close my eyes. The pain increases. I feel a hand caressing my forehead, over and over again. I open my eyes. There is complete darkness in the cave, and no one there.

WE MOVE very slowly on a swing made of rusting iron. The land far, then close again. Clouds move in the sky, covering the few stars. With his right arm Stefan pulls me close. The left is held up carefully in plaster and a sling. I look across the darkness in front of us and at the ridge of the rising hills. On the far side of the lawn a tall lamp throws down a yellow light that keeps shrinking into the evening as its voltage ebbs. My shoulder is padded and bandaged, my fractured wrist covered in a cast. Stefan pushes back with his legs and puts the swing into a faster motion. As we go higher we enter damp air.

"Did you think..."
"No. No, I..."
"Yes."
"How..."

"Those sculpted couples have everything to do with love."
"... the grown old stone."
"Tiny perforations."
"I wanted to..."
"So did I."
"Neither young nor old."

"That darkness, I couldn't..."
"I—"
"A monk..."
"A monk?"
"A monk..."

An owl calls, a radio plays far away, the temple bell rings, a fraudulent melancholy peace is created. I have known small towns like these living through the day only because one must wake with the light and go on, demolished by evening and its shrinking lightbulbs, yet never abandoning a guile perfected over centuries. Little remains of what was once elemental except a river or a line of hills that no one ever looks at. In the temples prayer resembles begging. In a barber's shop men look into stained mirrors for a long time and imagine themselves into being. And even then everything appears to be contained, continuous. What is knowable is what continues, not fractures, not human aberrations, what is knowable is a diseased eternity.

Near the weak yellow lamp there is a wooden table. A waiter with a face that never finds the world surprising, brings food on a tray that he holds high up in one raised hand. The waiter's expression does not change when he sees our arms and wrists in casts. He puts down the plates of food and glasses. He puts down two squat, used candles, a box of matches with some black grease on it. Stefan begins to arrange the food that the waiter has put down haphazardly. He lights the candles, positions the benches perfectly near the table, with his good arm. We sit facing each other, nocturnal selves that have left the daylight far behind.

It is a tensile night with no room in it for pity. I begin to eat, with a new hunger. A very old woman and a little girl are standing on the other side of the low wall that acts as a boundary to the lawn. I will love this man, I say to myself, despite my bruised, broken body, despite the raw desire alloyed with despair. The old woman is carrying a bunch of small yellow bananas. She wears a sari tied tightly to her body, without a blouse. She is thin and erect and strong. Below the table, Stefan stretches out his bare feet and encircles mine, tightly. His face is suddenly fragile. But it is a fragility that seems to have been there for years. What has happened in the day has only polished it and made it shine. The little girl has her hair very neatly combed and wears a dress that carries only a memory of printed flowers. It has been darned and stitched in many places, and the back is unbuttoned. Their gaze at us is constant and unflinching. There comes a regular thudding sound, loud, from not very far away, someone pulverizing an already beaten night. I look around to find its source. "An axe," Stefan says. "An axe on a strong tree trunk." This is the way things and people are placed next to one another now. Stefan and myself, like this, across from each other, us and the Padmapani, face to face, us, the boys and the Bodhistava.

There can be no equivalence between these things, between us, except the most elemental, for which we first have to be broken and excavated.

When it begins to rain we move inside. Light from the lamp outside falls in through the open windows. When Stefan kisses me I want to cry. I wanted this to be pure, unalloyed. He takes off my shirt. There are bruises and lacerations on my breasts. There is a large wound on the left which keeps oozing a viscous liquid. I touch his chest with my hands, the loosened skin, the slightly protruding stomach. He takes off my long skirt. He takes off his trousers. Then he takes me on his lap. The rain pelts our windows, the body pushes through the wreckage of the day.

"It wouldn't have happened if we weren't together," he says. His hands tremble.
In that near darkness our eyes are the only places that shine. I watch the lived years lodged in his face, his body. I see the expanded knowledge of things finding room, and emptiness moving from one place to another like a metastasis. The swirling wind pushes the rain through our windows and onto the dark floor. We lose the knowledge of who we are and our personal lives, age, youth, origin. I am strong enough to part the rain with my hands. We have recognised each other over centuries, we have only just met.

In the dawn spilling with light, I find myself sleeping with my head against Stefan's neck, sitting on his lap. He has held me there all night.

THE traveler drives through a large open plain, late at night. He stops the car, he turns off the lights. There are stars in the sky. Far away he sees two small lights, like tiny flames. As he walks towards it there are glimpses of silver. It is much further than it seemed at first, and he keeps walking. When he reaches, he sees it is a grave, covered with green cloth embroidered in silver, and above it a canopy made of red with a silver fringe, held up by four bamboo poles. Two oil lamps burn steadily on either side. There is no one nearby. He stands there listening to the cicadas. In the distance a man appears, with a basket on his head. He comes closer, and the traveler sees white jasmine. The man puts some flowers on the grave. The air becomes fragrant. Soon, another man comes, with a little boy holding a torn cloth bag. The man takes out tiny palm leaf fans from the bag. He lays down three on the grave. A third man appears with small sandalwood elephants. The fragrance of jasmine is interrupted by the sandalwood. He places an elephant on the grave. When the traveler looks into the night he sees men and women walking towards the grave, sellers of cloth who unfold a bolt over the grave, sellers of ribbons, bangles, embroidered dupattas, wooden beads. They kneel and lay down what they sell on the grave, then close their eyes and put their head on the green cloth. No one speaks. A cobbler arrives and lays down a hammer and a piece of leather. In the end, a monkey man comes with two emaciated monkeys. He puts one of them on the grave, and kneels down. The monkey sits there looking unsurprised. Suddenly he raises his knees, and puts his almost skeletal head on his withered arms.

The sellers leave as silently as they had come. They look at the traveler, neither accepting him, nor rejecting him. When they have left, he goes close to the grave covered with flowers and objects made by hand. He would like to put his head on the grave but he cannot. He would like to put his hand on the grave but he cannot. He would like to be as open as this dark plain. He would like to travel outside his life.

LANDSCAPES

THE AIRPLANE travels from west to east, moving towards night. It is not the light leaving as on earth, but the light being left behind, the sky a transparent blue, lit by a gold so diminished that it has turned into darkened silver and become as fragile as light can be, while continuing to enable sight. When it reaches that which is human, it refracts through flesh and bone, alters the human course of things. What remains is breath, long, what remains is gaze, longer. This light is a serene vigilance, though it has nothing to protect, for it can never be wounded, or seized, or injured and then stitched together, like skin on a face; it is attention unceasing, and for as long as the light lasts it refracts the human into an equal consciousness. Then the aircraft passes into night. That light, unforgotten, was made from the residues of the left behind sun. In Sanskrit, residue is *shesha*, the remainder, left over from actions, numbers, desires. To someone for whom this language is an ancestor, its words interrogate other languages, makes them tensile. The discontinuous is rarely to be found, even the spinning of the earth a residue from a larger rotation of a cloud of matter that collapsed into planets. A dead mother, not loving, not loved, appears one day in the mirror in my own body. Not in shape or feature, because we do not resemble one another. She appears only in the flow of blood and the posture of muscles behind the raised eyes as I look at my reflection in passing, the intent of the shoulder above an awkwardly lifted arm, an abrupt turning of the head to look at something that does not concern me, new movements, and this only after the mother's death, never before, the mother now as remainder, and as remainder more in me than she ever was, with no way for me to refuse. The mother had been a widow and lived as a widow for twenty four years. Absences crowded what she insisted was her heart. The absence of the loving husband, the obedient child. The widow that appears on the avenue is not light skinned, sharp featured, or in the starched cotton saris of the mother with pleats so sharp they can draw blood. This widow wears a white sari that is limp, it has been worn so much that it is as soft as silk, no longer really white, draped without pleats, all the way around her head and her blouseless chest. She is dark-skinned, old, she is thin and barefoot, she is unprotected and strong. I drive by her on the broad avenue with ornate buildings and homes from the nineteenth century, almost European, an avenue she has no reason to ever stand on. I sing an old Bengal song, of a night when the storm breaks down the doors of a home, and as I pass by her she stops me. She brings her face close and looks inside the car, taking some time to focus her faded eyes, she says how moving this song, how beautiful the way you sing it. Come with me she says and I leave the car behind and walk with her, and behind the avenue is another street with small houses under corrugated iron roofs and in one of them she takes me in and offers me, in the sweating shadows, coconut sweets on a timeless, dented bell metal plate. She is no one I have ever met before, but we are not strangers. "I'm so far away from home here," she says, "this is all I have to give you." She means a few hundred miles and perhaps a river. She means the other side of Bengal. For her the land does not stretch to form a subcontinent. She is herself and all those women who wore only white after their husbands died, widows spawned by early marriage, mothers, grandmothers, aunts, maidservants, hawkers of rice, not eating cooked food on the eleventh day of the lunar fortnight, not eating fish or meat, garlic or onions, banned from welcoming the bridegroom at weddings, rarely to be pitied, almost always equal to the suffering forced upon them. Her hands tremble and she holds the plate slanting down towards me sitting on the floor, I straighten it, but it slants again. Then she brings a bowl of gur, that too at an angle so I can see the depth of the bowl, and finally a glass of water in a large bell metal glass that shines like gold, the water slanting to the brim, but nothing, not even the water, falls, or spills or drops. She gives me what I can taste, eat and digest, food that the cells in my body remember over centuries, and I attain a precarious nourishment.

I have just returned from a place where everything was as it should be, only children and parents in the playground, linden trees on the avenues, the Ishtaar Gate in the museum, the past in the past.

Here, behind the street on which the widow lives, rice fields begin. Across the harvested brown fields with stumps of paddy, the only things laid out in straight lines, there are groves of trees, homes, ponds. The falling light

touches the surface of a pond, darkened by the shadows of trees that surround it. At this time here, after harvest, the light is more golden, more in-
fused with red than in any other season. No matter how far I travel I will
have to return here, or rather, it will return to me, it will come to me un-
bidden, take me by surprise. Pieces of land begin to grow from the air and
water in the body, islands with bamboo groves and afternoons float on my
circulating blood, the land changes with the seasons, there are fathers under trees watching these seasons pass, there are grandmothers with wrinkled hands, there are wishes that are sown into the soil without concern
for fulfillment, and adulthood is not reached by keeping out what came before. That which has not yet come, *anagata*, includes that which existed a
very long time ago. I did not move from those ponds and groves to the city.
I have never lived in those homes among ponds, groves and rivers. I want
to return where I have never been.

A BOATMAN, *standing as he rows, turns to look back at the man he is ferry-*
ing, exactly at the moment when tears gather in the man's eyes. The man sits at
the other end of the small, narrow boat. The leaving light burnishes his gathered
tears. The boatman always has his back towards those he ferries. All the more
every traveler, thinking himself alone with river and sky, surrenders to the move-
ments of his own heart. The boatman perceives those movements even with his
back turned.
"Swallow it," the boatman says. "Like Neelkantha."
The man looks up, unsurprised, and holds the look. It is, the boatman feels, an
accusation. Then the man drops his eyes towards the planks of the narrow boat,
and he sees the boatman's bare legs and feet covered with eczema, red and raw, a
few points emitting small drops of blood. The man thinks of his destination, his
beautiful wife, her skin like milk touched by rose, waiting for him in her parents'
home. She can give him nothing—even the way she combs her own long hair is
without love. And yet he has to be her husband, bear her life.

On these rivers wide as seas there were long times without shores, nothing human except the boat moving.

"You're telling me to swallow my own fate," the man says.

"Can you question the river?"

"You can question what creates your fate."

The boatman loosens his grip on the oars. The boat drifts on the current instead of moving ahead. The man waits, without impatience. The sunset gold falls very precisely over both of them, over the boat and the stretch of water before them, holding them in a last refulgence that scoops them out of time's flow.

When the light begins to pull away, and darkness rises from the surface of the water, the boatman takes up the oars once again. The man, returning from the city, prepares for land, for the recrudescence of his everyday life among people settled on this earth for centuries. They have rested their bodies on this land, grown their food, planted their rituals deep, till the place where soil met rock. He would always be a husband to this wife. Would it ever be possible to live more than one life, to change course, to at least move towards one's possibilities? The traveler is born of thought, even before actual movement. It has been ten years, and his wife has not conceived a child. But if he does have a child, and it is a daughter, he will love her enough to make her a traveler, so that she can choose what must move, and what should stay in place.

The boatman rows for a long time, but there is still no shore in sight. There is, at a distance, a small green island on which there is a single hut. When the boat comes close to it, the boatman says, "Can we rest here?"

The man hesitates for a moment, then steps onto land. In the hut a man is sculpting an image of Durga, the pujas only a month away. It is unfinished, as yet the colour of the gray dark river clay from which it has been made, unpainted, unadorned. The eyes are not yet opened, the ten hands are all formed to grasp the weapons that will be put in them at the end, but for now, holding only air. The image maker rounds out a nipple. Later the fresh, bright paint, the sholapith and tinsel jewellery will cover this nakedness, and this life. The adornments *will hide the aetiology of this faith that comes from a land of excess exceeding it-self, brimming harvests from pouring rain that brings floods and death, and the utterly fertile silt that is left behind by the floodwaters that will in turn seed more harvests and provide the river mud and clay that this image is made of. The ritu-als of the puja will settle over the body, the eyes will judge the worshippers. The man sits down in the dark shed. The image maker looks at him for a moment then turns back to his work. Sweat runs down his face. Here, in something form-ing and not yet formed, something not yet made but still in the making, in the unfinished, there is hope.*

"Water?" asks the image maker, without taking his hands off the clay.

The boatman sits on the edge of the land looking out.

When they begin to move again, darkness has long covered river and sky. The man lies down on one end of the boat, watching the water go by. He doesn't know when it is that he falls asleep. When he wakes up it is dawn. He sits up and looks at the boatman.

"I only wanted to go to the other shore," he says.

"I've been rowing all night," the boatman replies, "and only at dawn can I see that I'm still in the same place."

This is what I see, an unknown boatman, and a man who is not yet, but will be, my father, both on a river I have never seen. It is not a memory, it never hap-pened. It is a refraction of that which did.

———

THE only thing from the city that hangs suspended in my body is a long balcony hovering over the night, a moonless night, the darkest in the year, and a hundred and eight candles burn on the balcony's ledge. I have put them there myself, along with cousins and aunts, lighting every new can-dle with the previous one, and using the dripping wax from the flame to stand it in place. An image of Kali goes by on the street below, moving to-wards the river on the edges of the city, and I can look from where I stand into her carefully created eyes. The night has the consistency of mist, sometimes the mist collapses into early evening, and I look down from the balcony to see who stands at the main door below, ringing the sharp door-bell. It could be an aunt, a cousin, a distant uncle, a neighbour, a father's playmate from childhood, a grandmother's partner in prayer, the purohit for Lakshmi puja, the arranger of marriages, the second cousin of a father who comes here to stay and coughs up blood for a year while he comes slowly back to health, the old man from next door who is grandfather to every child in the neighbourhood, the boy who loves the young girl of the house but will never be able to express it and will marry someone else, from the balcony an aerial view of human relationships, too numerous to name, forming its own landscape of difficult terrains and firm grounds, and accepted as a landscape must be accepted.

Landscapes open in the empty self, and those never traveled to equal those one was born from. The one never traveled to unrolls inch by inch, a few hours at a time, from right to left. White mulberry trees must grow and mature, bear leaves that the silkworm will feed on, the worm will spin its silk, the silk will be spun again into fabric, and this will be pounded and smoothened for making landscapes on. Mountains will then be imagined, and rivers, skies. Mist will be made by keeping the texture of the silk untouched. The body expands to hold twisted trees close by on the left, stretches far ahead into the foreground to include water moving over rocks and stones and away between hills to a reticent sunset sky. The near, the far and the infinite have the same illumination. Only densities separate mountain and cloud. This is a landscape of adulthood, it has too much space for a child. It is for the self emptied out, for the face that has been injured, for the person who has little that is personal. Moving left the hills rise into austere mountains, coming forth and receding, trees appear, twisted, bent, water comes and goes, everything unfolding towards a river spreading all the way to clouds and sky. Anxiety is the impossibility of dreaming and therefore of being unbound. The light here is made from the setting of the sun and the brown gold silk that contains within it a recessed illumination, like hesitant daylight, distilled from the light of the universe. The empty self, already ragged, threadbare, is able to let go the craving for the personal and become anonymous.

The surgeon stitches the skin on my face, closing what has burst open. He raises his needle up and back in again. "I'm doing the first layer now," he tells me. At the end of a layer he finishes with a knot, and wipes away the blood. "I'll have to do three layers," he says. "Did someone push her?" the surgeon's assistant asks. "No, she fell," he says. The assistant, disappointed, says not a single word after that. She arranges scissors, needles, and scalpels on a steel tray. The dark space I fall through each time has no signs by which I can recognise it the next time I am on its edge. It is composed of nothing, a created darkness, that unlike any real one, has no access to light.

Light is harvested as the year turns, winter light from months of indiscriminate blazing, a blue sky from a colourless expanse, a thinner air from the one that weighed down the paving stones. Light that can now be felt as light, separate from the atmosphere. Where I live the sea is now restrained, drawn back from the shore, the fishing boats expansive, going far, the skin pulling in. After dark oil lamps, candles, stars, lights strung on the dark shapes of trees, a greater silence. The seven strings of yellow light that move up from a wide base and meet at a point above, to form a quiet tree, throw their light on the face of the chowkidar at the gate. In the evening, moving through the streets, going towards the reticent blue lights strung on old cottages in need of repair, being reached by the brighter incandescence of the yellow and the white hung high across a narrow lane, discovering a cluster of red stars hidden among dusty bushes, watching the light inside churches as I pass, from the entrance all the way to the candles at the altar, I watch what moves and what holds still, receiving light as light, not greater than anything, not opposed to anything, not even darkness. In the distances opened up by what never existed, light travels far, and moving, is an indication, an upward rising assurance. No light is excessive here, paper stars of light hung from temporary wires, strings of lights bought at the hardware shop backed by a broken corrugated iron sheet painted white, lights held up with ropes and bamboo poles, not dim, but mortal. They must be found in the darkness. Light that is made, and so can be torn and broken, set in the darkness that comes and goes without human effort. This is earnt. That light lit in certain seasons only, the correct ones. That is earnt. The unstable as a reply to the stable, that is earnt.

There is the deepest rest in the other's breath in the darkness of dawn. There is a permanence in the street outside with its new interlocking paver stones. Beneath it is the land's undertow, pulling away .

In places that are forgotten, the sky goes back a few hundred years, then a thousand, then a thousand and eight hundred. It holds up a ruined fort, presses through the stone lattice work of mausoleums, watches from a shaded pavilion. Only sometimes does the land bear a fort, a mosque, a stupa, a line of caves. Otherwise it is empty except for barren hills and scrub. A young boy quietly gathers fallen leaves and dust inside the grounds of a dargah, his left arm folded over his bent back. The caretaker sits still on a mat and watches the scrub tremble a little in the wind. In the large courtyard of a mosque, five men sit in a line on the verandah without speaking. In one corner Aurangzeb's small marble tomb is enclosed by white walls. Two young men sweep the courtyard from opposite ends, looking up from time to time at the empty sky. There are no birds here, the sound of sweeping from brooms made of dry reeds fills the silence. The dome inside the mosque is deep black, made from bats clinging tightly to the concave surface together, each bat fitted to the body of another so completely that an even black covers the original pattern of indigo and white. Men attain a stillness here, its source apparently a crippling patience. Only the most necessary actions are performed. The man who guards shoes at the entrance squats on the ground and studies the space between his bare, cracked feet. The visitor will never know if the empty sky has subjugated these men all their lives, or if the landscape has given its life to the undying mausoleums and not to those with shorter life spans. Not so far from here, in the caves, stone Buddhas teach stillness. The borders between this stillness and stasis, both evolved over centuries, are hard to define. Outside the mosque the land is undulating, and on each of the three small hills there is a mausoleum of carefully carved stone. Stars burst from the darkness inside them through the lattice work of the windows, flowers and leaves form the arches over the doorways. Real weeds and plants sprout through every opening, tufts of scrub emerge from the domes. The wind comes in sharp gusts, talking only to itself. They say there are fifteen hundred Sufi saints buried here, in this stretch of land, in the useless scrub, most of them under a plain slab of stone, which the scrub and weeds may have covered forever. They began to come here in the tenth century from Persia along the routes of trade. There are Sufis buried here from the many different schools, the Nakshbandi, Suhrawardiyya, Qadiriyyah, Chistiya, Shattaria, Razak Shahi, Khaksari, Mohkam Shahi, Jan Alla Shahi, Rafa, Biabani, Madaria and Tabkati, and Sufis who traveled only on their own path.

Beyond the mausoleums the land rises into a high hill and then falls away into the valley below. When people who have come from far away enter here, they begin to move in every direction, not knowing which way to go. The sun has lowered itself into the valley and the endless sky is wrinkled with bands of gleaming crimson. Someone hurriedly climbs the hill. This land has been ploughed over and over by faith. Someone rushes into a ruined mausoluem. This land has been ploughed over and over by defiance. Someone stands rooted in the scrub. This land has been ploughed over and over by a defiance born of faith. The visitors lose their intent. They lose all their carefully built bonds of intellect, friendship, even a shared past, they become solitary, brought back to a primeval aloneness. Truncated cries float in the sunset air. Extreme exhalations swell the wind. There is nothing for the outsider to do, restore, write down, remake. There is no lament in the land. Each man made thing here has been brutal, above all to itself.

The visitors will not leave till it is completely dark, they will slip and fall while picking their way through the scrub, they will tear their hands and feet on thorns.

Children emerge suddenly from a minuscule settlement at the base of the hill, girls and boys about to reach adolescence. They shout across the wind and call the visitor, "Didi, Didi." They don't walk up to the tomb, but stand near their homes and call. "Didi," they go on. "Come here Didi, we want to ask you some questions." The visitor sits down on the plinth, facing away from the houses. They go on calling, "Don't you have any children?" "Don't you?" The wind moves through the empty sky, sometimes elongating their chant, "Don't you..." and sometimes breaking the chant down to one single word, "Children."

Two young men drive up here on motorcycles, gaze for a few minutes at the setting sun and then, disillusioned, drive away. The road from here winds down along the hillside on the right, the valley on the left. Where the road becomes flat and the hills curve in to the right, there the Ellora caves begin.

A BULL comes down from the sky. He sits at the entrance of a cave, his legs gathered on the right, his body leaning left, facing the darkness inside, at rest and ready to move any moment, as epochs go by. Light from the sky enters the caves on its hands and knees. As a consequence, the stone floor is precarious with wrinkles, craters, swellings. Feet walk on this stone. The feet that stop, that revolve suddenly, slowly, in one place, are the feet that the stone recognises. To begin by carving from a rock standing by itself, then carving on the flank of a mountainside, epochs passing. Perhaps all the time considering how to go further, another age gone by. The originary vision will submit only to elemental laws, the rising of the sun, the coming of the rains, the turning of the hills from brown to green and back again. Otherwise, it is ruthless and single minded. To penetrate rock and arrive inside, to a singular darkness, using hammer and chisel, and iron rods, and years. To stand in the marrow of the originary. Not only to penetrate a mountain, but to scoop it out, to pull the sky in from above. Attacking these hills formed from the oldest, most resistant rock in the land. Not a submissive moment, except to pause for breath, and lay aside all tools when darkness comes. The new is rigorous and brutal. From one end of a cave corridor, looking at Durga on the far wall—the face has the levity of a smile. The light widens her opened pelvis. Walking towards, the smile begins to change, the face admits thought. Very close, at her feet, looking up, the face turns serious, it takes on the world. On the axis of this movement, from far to near, there is no place on which to position a universal truth. In a corner, where the sun never reaches, in the privacy of shadows, they stand together hand on hand, her head tilted towards him, his bending towards her, her left foot on her right, the left toe pressing down to hold in what is moving inside her. Outside there are the regal elephants, the vigilant lions, the flying apsaras on the higher walls, the unbridled sunlight, the spreading sky, the world turning. To change the properties of rock, to first make it pneumatic, then to set it in motion with its own breath. There is no place for the individual here. Moving in from light to darkness, the individual is made numerous by the many pillars, scattered among the gods, animals, apsaras, and demons, flattened by the massiveness of bare, vertical rock and, emerging again, nullified by the endless sky. The modern, the contemporary, the future, looking forward, looking westward, looking eastward from the westward, the modern, the inventions, the communications now possible, the travel, the airborne, machines emitted into space, cables under seas. There are places in the caves where light never arrives. The insolence of shadows, their defiance of light. The ten-armed, the skeleton, the one-breasted, the ten-headed, the limbs folded in flight, the man-lion, caring nothing for anyone's gaze. They come forth from the deepest recesses of the rock. They twist, spin, kill, dance, kneel, bend over, not a moment in time arrested, but as continuous condition. They come forth in a direction diagonal to the passing of time. These caves, abandoned for centuries, return to the watcher a gaze uninterrupted by ritual, return the human to an elemental tenderness. The couples sit, embedded into small squares on pillars, or on large niches in walls, rarely looking at each other, resting their seated bodies, their palms, on the plinth of love. They have gone past the looking at each other, into each other, not past love, but the anxiety of loving. The attention is now turned towards the outside and so they look far, not as one, but as two resting on the one base of love, they consider the world, together. Their limbs are always awkward, the woman's foot on the man's thigh, or the man holding the wrist of the woman, not the hand. These gestures may be either an artist's mistake that proved correct, or intended by an artist who knew the consequences. The bodies going outside intention, adjusting their positions as they turn, continuously, from loving to contemplation. On the ledge of a cave, blinded by the light. The sky occupies more space here than anywhere else in the known world, circular like the earth. An awning of bare rock hangs over the ledge, careless and curving in places as if it were windblown cloth. To have studied light, to have studied shadows, to have studied the rain, in this way to have understood motion, in this way to have understood change, in this way to have come upon the fact that nothing remains the same, in this way to create something and leave it, leaving it to the light, leaving it to shadows, leaving it, even, to the rains, leaving it to its contradictions. A man is about to say goodbye before he returns to a country far away. When he embraces his friend he is tall, lean, straight, middle-aged. As he turns around and bends down to pick up his two bags he becomes an old man, and as he walks towards the entrance of the airport he takes small steps, shuffling forward like someone in the last years of his life. Knowing distilled from the elements, made elemental. In the evening, oil lamps may reveal no gestures, only limbs, not a hand but the weapon held. A man holds himself in, always. He is felled by unknown assailants. From his hospital bed, his arms cannot stop extending out, his hands hold the face of a friend and will not let it go. The friend keeps her face there, her neck stretched across his body, like an artist's mistake, or intention. Not a moment of submission. Every figure that comes forth from the rock has the energy and weight of its source, its massiveness. The tender appears like a miracle, marrow in bone. From the carving of a rock standing alone, to breaking open a hillside and carving the darkness, a millennium. The new reconstitutes the land, it is geological, it takes its time.

THEY left behind nothing that could be grasped by the hand, or walked on by feet. Not a monument, a coin, a jewel, a weapon. From the time of the Aryans, coming in small waves across the Hindu Kush mountains, till the time of the Buddha, not a palace, a seal, a bowl. Only a vigilance, the conjugations and declensions of words, a stamina for the infinite. The infinite had the patience of the loom, the tenacity of the plough, the consistency of iron. The horse on the street stands quietly for hours, tethered to a lamp post. It has infinity in its eyes. The past is not subject to the laws of perspective. It is not discovered at a point in the distance where pieces of knowledge meet. It is forthcoming. Words are read under the lamplight. It has been hard work under the lamplight, it has been hard work to acquire the lamplight. The horse's breath moves the dark leaves outside. Nomads who crossed the mountains on horseback, and those who were already farming the land, perhaps began to see, over centuries, that things standing will fall, but the moving forever stay.

For the postman, or the one giving directions, the street is a cul-de-sac, with a small church on a rising slope at the end. But for the one who lives here it is a world closed off on one side, open at the other. What comes in can be considered over a longer time, understood by the echoes it leaves behind. Hymns flow down the slope from the church and collide with the call of the knife sharperner on his last rounds. The coucal flies low, spreading its large, rust coloured wings in the undergrowth. Labourers drill the penultimate niche in a new apartment and in the three storied building a woman and her daughter talk to two robust policemen and say, "Only because we are two women here alone…" The rest of her sentence is covered by the sound of the fruit seller coming in with his call, trying to steer his heavy cart around the seven stray dogs being fed from plastic containers by a devastated woman with a concave body and a dented face.

They sang hymns in praise of the sun, they asked for a full harvest, even more they asked the sun for its luminosity, its intelligence. That, after all, would be more dependable. They looked so long, hundreds and hundreds of years, that they saw the attributes of each thing, and then threw away the idea of attributes like husk from grain. They could describe something by the qualities it did not possess. They arrived at this not from a lack, but from navigating the surfeit of things, light, crops, rivers. It is not possible to know what they intended, what they did not, what they overlooked. The gaze that is now directed towards them has its own desires, its own errors.

A woman sits, her right thigh on her lover's lap, her head against his warm neck, his hair, she sits on the plinth of love, looking out at the early morning, the tiny yellow warbler moving on the window ledge, the trees so various beyond, and the two of them silent, still rising. The street has attributes, but these must be forgotten. Sounds that emerge from the street are reflected off the slope, and magnified, holding for a long time. On an unusual day a brass band moves towards the church with a hearse. The air is slashed every day by pneumatic drills, stone polishing machines, tiles being torn off floors, debris being loaded on to trucks, nine street dogs fighting all night. As soon as dawn comes, the birds begin their calls, and the dogs fall silent. But the street's silence is not made only of matter. A woman lives on the plinth, the equilibrium of love, and this in turn stands on the poise of the street. No matter what, the street tends, always, towards homeostasis, helped by a physiology between hill and sea. Before the street appeared, this land was fields of rice. Before the rice fields, and perhaps before the invention of agriculture, it was a fisherman's coast. Before it was coast it was land joined to another continent. There are no places to be gone to, everything is here, in the same way that the turned away eyes of the Bodhisatva Padmapani do not need to see more, more detail, more facts, more nuances, more variousness. In the afternoon, a golden oriole moves from branch to branch.

In the late twilight of summer the birdcalls are many and complex, they echo through the trees as if this were a rainforest. It was once. It brings longing for a real forest, but appeases it at the same time. Early in the morning as the yellow and olive warbler returns to the window, the rising couple hears a fight two buildings away, the voice of a woman shouting, and then a man saying, "I'm *tired* of..." after which the wind disperses the syllables, and the one word, *tired*, hangs in the quiet air, because it was the most forceful word uttered, and every heart that hears it feels the irrefutable truth of his tiredness, the days and months and years behind it. Is he more tired or as much or less than the labourers who repair the roof of a cottage, spending all day in the difficult May sun, without a single piece of shade? They cover their heads with a cloth, and work using hammer and chisel and a spade. Above them parrots fly hurriedly in pairs. The older man who leads says to one of them, "Break it gently." The younger man looks up for a moment at the blinding light and closes his eyes, then goes back to his work. At sundown, the labourers, covered in gravel and dust, wash only their faces at the small tap and head homeward.

The seasons have passed, the roof that the labourers were working on is repaired, and it is winter. The mango trees bear small, gray lizard eggs on their trunks. For a month now, till the winter solstice, the darkness will come early, a rare reprieve from the need to oppose incessant light. Thresholds and windows are more defined, not melting into the outside. I was pushed towards beauty so hard that I fell on my face, and bear the scar under my left eye. I have seen others pushed even harder, so that their vision was taken away. A flawed solitude takes refuge at windows, thresholds and doors. They are as unsure as I am, but will die only after I do. Outside is the vacant plot, overgrown with weeds, and trees that have risen high over many monsoons. Unknown birds live amongst their leaves. Night rises from the ground here, before it appears anywhere else. That is why the yellow light bulb comes on early in the small corrugated iron shed where night watchmen live among the weeds. The darkness then rises to the small church on the slope and clings to the hymns being sung inside. It allows the candles to burn steadily on the church steps, and then moves among the crowns of various trees on the slope. Beauty is not an attribute of matter. The matter that makes this night and what it contains is for the watcher beautiful, though it needs to be remade each time. The night here contains the elsewhere, the forest, the wilderness. It holds things long gone from the earth. The watcher sees the near and the far, as alert as the moon that passes across this sky diagonally each night, late or early according to the season. It is an immense night, continuous with the universe.

My mother walks towards my door. I stand at the threshold and watch her as she walks, closer to me with every slow step, her face severe, disapproving of me, of the whole world, of the way the planets move. She leans on a gray metal crutch from a recent fall, the young nurse follows her. She wears a starched tangail sari as she always does, and she is able to make even a sari an instrument of hurt, the starch so stiff that my skin cuts in places where my hands brush against it, in the rare times that I am close to her body. She approaches me, my open door, and there is terror in my heart, because I can never be prepared for the ways in which she will strike, cut, and wound me. She comes closer, and the nurse comes closer, and the nurse is smiling, but not me or my mother, and I try to prepare myself but I can't, and the few people who understand something of this say to me, "It's only a few hours." Even they don't know that these hours are only when the terror is physically proximate, but that it has existed eternally, like the wind or the sky, and is able to strike from a great distance.

My mother walks with her sharp sari slowly into the immensity, resting her crutch on this night, but the crutch falls through without anything to support it, and her pleats can wound nothing, because the night has no substance and she disappears, swallowed by the night, drenched in dark saliva and masticated.

It is an immense night, continuous with the universe. The same immensity that the doctor brings before me when he speaks about the age of the earth. He speaks of the formation of coastlines, the ancient rocks on the ocean floor. He knows that the immense is practical, useful. The same immensity waits outside elevator doors. It swallows those with the tongues of beggars who lick at the appearances of things. I am the night and I watch the night. My dead father is part of this immensity, not as a face or a body, but broken down into atoms and become part of the darkness and air. Nothing truly loved retains its form, its boundaries. The man I will be with forever lives behind doors and windows, but the indestructible matter in him stretches and is attenuated so far that it becomes, like the night, pre-human.

A scrawny goddess comes out of the night, with fifteen arms, nine on the left and six on the right, arms that are long and thin, stretching far beyond her body. Three of these arms are bent at the elbow and raised over her head, like the antlers of a large insect. She has only one leg, the right, and that is enough to let her stand on the darkness. Her body is black-brown, her belly protruding from the rest of her thinness, and her open breasts are scrunched together. The arms came one by one as they were needed, to fight back, to threaten, to shove, to strangle. They did not exist when she was born. She may yet grow a few more. There are always new things to attack, to protect, to tear out from the universe. Someone may have broken her leg, and thrown her away as refuse, but she returned from the darkness behind the huts and trees, her new arms and the one leg all balancing each other. Now, if she was pushed to the ground, she could walk on her many hands. This is an immense night, continuous with the universe.

KEY HINDI AND BENGALI WORDS

bandhni: a kind of tie and dye fabric; *brun*: hard, round bread; *dargah*: a structure which holds the tomb of a saint; *dupatta*: a long scarf worn by Indian women with a kurta; *ghada*: a large clay pitcher for water; *gur*: jaggery; *Irani*: a neighbourhood café; *jali*: lattice work; *kolsi*: a large clay pitcher for water; *matka*: a large clay pitcher for water; *mochi*: cobbler, usually from a low caste; *Neelkantha*: A form of the God Shiva in which he drinks poison and holds it in his throat so it turns blue; *pir*: saint; *pujari*: a temple priest; *pujas*: the ritual of worshipping a god or goddess; *purohit*: a Hindu priest for rituals of worship; *randi*: whore; *rudra veena*: one of the oldest stringed instruments in Indian classical music; *surya namskar*: a series of yoga asanas; *swabhava*: nature; *Swami Haridas*: said to be Tansen's music guru; *tanpura*: a four-stringed drone instrument; *Tansen*: a great singer in the court of the medieval Mughal emperor Akbar; *urs*: death anniversary of a Sufi saint.

IMAGES

Pg.54, Detail from a Folio of the Gita Govinda Series, identified as Pg.36 above

Pg.58, Detail from a Gita Govinda Folio
c. 1775-80
Attributed to a Master of the First Generation after Nainsukh
Private Collection

Pg.59, Detail from a Gita Govinda Folio
1775-80
Attributed to the First Generation after Nainsukh
The Kronos Collection, New York

Pg.59, Detail from Shiva and His Family on Mount Kailash

Pg.60, Earthrise, Apollo 8, NASA

CITY

Detail of Bodhisatva Padmapani photograph
from the Ajanta Caves *by Benoy Behl*
Gulmohur, *Sharmistha Mohanty*

CAVES

Photograph of Bodhisatva Padmapani *by Benoy Behl*
Couple from the Ajanta Caves, *Sharmistha Mohanty*

LANDSCAPES

Photographs courtesy *Samimitra Das*

ACKNOWLEDGMENTS

Excerpts from this book have appeared in *Almost Island, Drunken Boat, Gallerie, Jintian, Pratilipi* and *The Caravan*.

Parts of this work were written during a residency at Yaddo in the United States.

My deep gratitude to Vahni Capildeo for her close reading of the manuscript. Vivek Narayanan's reading of the drafts, and his suggestions, have meant a great deal.

To all the museums on different continents which have so kindly made original images of the miniature paintings available to me, my heartfelt thanks. I would not have been able to reproduce these images at their best without the help of Dr. Eberhard Fischer and Jorrit Britschgi of the Museum Rietberg; Dr. B.N. Goswamy; the Government Museum and Art Gallery, Chandigarh; Steven Kossak and the Kronos Collection.

Thanks also to Namit Arora for making his photographs available.

To Itu Chaudhuri, for being there, my gratefulness.

Pg. 40, from *Richard Wagner: The Man, His Mind and His Music, Mariner Books, 1990*

SHARMISTHA MOHANTY is the author of two previous works of fiction—*Book One* and *New Life*. She has also translated a selection of Tagore's fictional work, *Broken Nest and Other Stories*.

Mohanty is founder-editor of the online journal *Almost Island* and the initiator of the *Almost Island Dialogues*, an annual international writers meet held in New Delhi.

Her writing has been impacted by several years in the United States—she studied fiction at the Iowa Writers Workshop—learning and talking with some rare writers, among them her mentor at Iowa, James Alan McPherson. Ironically, it was at Iowa that she was also taught by U.R.Ananthamurthy, who brought to some young Indian writers there the charged works of Ashis Nandy among others. Mohanty has been influenced by her long involvement with film—a medium in which she has worked and interacted with some of its finest practitioners—directors, cinematographers, editors, and sound designers. She wrote the script for *Nazar*, working with the profound director Mani Kaul, with whom she had an on-going dialogue for over twenty years till his death in 2011. She has also been a student of *Dhrupad* under Bahauddin Dagar.

Mohanty is the recipient of several fellowships, including one at the Akademie Schloss Solitude in Germany, as well as a Senior Fellowship from the Ministry of Culture in India.

She is currently on the International Faculty of the Creative Writing MFA programme at the City University of Hong Kong.

She lives in Mumbai.